FIVE ROUNDS

JAMES P. SUMNER

BOTH
barrels
PUBLISHING

DISCLAIMER

The short stories (known as *One-Shots*) that follow were originally published as individual titles exclusive to the author's own website, and were only available as eBooks.

Here, they have been collected for the first time and published via mainstream platforms in both digital and print formats. Consequently, they are no longer available individually from the author's website.

Please note: aside from an updated edit to polish some of the older content, the stories themselves remain unchanged.

A few quick hits...

FORGED

AN ADRIAN HELL ONE-SHOT

JUNE 16, 2003

1

I hear footsteps just outside the bedroom. A creaking floorboard dragged me from my sleep. It tripped the alarm buried deep inside my subconscious, set to go off if any of the built-in warnings are triggered.

I open my eyes and quickly run a mental assessment. My gun is locked inside a metal box on the top shelf of my closet. The key is in the drawer of the nightstand beside me. I check the time. It's light outside, so there's no way to use darkness as an element of surprise.

Being careful not to make any noise, I push myself up in bed, so I'm sitting upright against the headboard. The only option here is to be direct.

"I can hear you out there," I say, keeping my voice at little more than a whisper. "I'm giving you one chance..."

The door bursts open. The sound of laughter fills the room.

"Daddy!"

A smile spreads across my face as my daughter runs toward me. She jumps on the bed, between me and her mom, and buries her head in my chest.

I wrap my arms around her and hold her tight.

"Hey, sweetie." I kiss the top of her head. "You're getting good at sneaking up on us."

Maria looks up at me, her blue eyes wide with excitement. "Really, Daddy?"

I chuckle. "Hell yeah. I hardly heard you that time. You're like a ninja!"

I poke her tummy and she giggles.

"Stop it!"

Beside her, my wife, Janine, rolls over on her back and stretches. She props herself up on her elbow and snakes her arm around Maria's waist, pulling her toward her.

"Has my monkey been creeping up on us again?" she asks playfully before pretending to eat her neck.

Maria giggles.

Janine looks at me and smiles. It's as if a spotlight just shone down on her face. She's the most beautiful woman I've ever seen in my life.

"Hey, handsome," she says.

I lean over and kiss her forehead. "Hey, yourself. Sleep okay?"

"I sure did." She lies Maria down between us. "And what about you, sweetie? Did you sleep well?"

My baby girl nods exaggeratedly. "I did, Mommy. But I couldn't wait to get up this morning, so I can go to school!"

She's been in pre-school since September, but she considers it *actual* school. She loves to learn.

I raise an eyebrow. "What kind of a crazy monster are you? And what have you done with my daughter?"

She starts hitting my arm. "It's me, Daddy! I'm not a monster!"

I laugh, pretending her punches hurt. "Then quit beating me up!"

She giggles again. It's from the belly and sounds infectious and genuine. It's the kind of child-like laugh you can't help but smile at.

"Now get outta here, monkey. Your mom gets cranky if she doesn't get chance to beat me up before going to work."

Janine reaches over and punches me, which hurts more than Maria's efforts. "Adrian!"

She smiles and shakes her head.

Maria laughs. "I'm gonna go get dressed for school."

She bounces along the bed, then drops off the end and runs out of the room. She starts running along the hall, but quickly backtracks to close our bedroom door.

The second it clicks shut, Janine's on me like a predator. She straddles my waist, resting her hands on my chest.

"I like beating you up, do I?" she asks with a menacing glint in her eyes.

"I think that's what the kids are calling it nowadays, yeah," I reply, smiling.

"Well..." She leans forward and kisses me. "...you're gonna have to wait for your sparring session, soldier. I have a meeting this morning, before my shift starts."

She dismounts and pads over to the bathroom. Her vest top and panties do very little to cover her body, which I will never complain about.

I roll out of bed and drop to the floor, completing my morning routine of thirty push-ups before getting dressed. Janine reappears as I'm fastening my jeans.

"Put a shirt on," she says with a wry smile. "You're not impressing anybody."

Since being officially discharged from the service six months ago, I've tried to maintain the shape it got me in—something my wife is happy about, regardless of how cool she tries to play it.

"Baby, please..." I tense my stomach and arms. "You know you love it."

She says nothing but winks at me, silently promising trouble later tonight.

I pull a thin, black sweater over my head. "See you downstairs."

08:42 EDT

Most people, if they walked into their kitchen in the morning to see a strange man feeding eggs to their daughter, would be alarmed. But for me, this happens almost every day.

Maria looks over and smiles. The man scraping scrambled eggs onto her plate looks over too.

"Morning, sweetie," he says. "Breakfast?"

I roll my eyes. "No, thanks, Josh."

We bump fists as I sit down at the table next to Maria. "You're early."

He pours himself a coffee and rests against the counter, cradling the mug in his hand. "Yeah, we have that... *appointment* this morning, remember?"

What appointment?

My eyes narrow as I access my memory, trying to think what he—

Oh, yeah.

I remember.

I look at him and nod.

Now it's his turn to roll his eyes. "There we go." He looks at Maria. "Your old man has the worst memory *ever!*"

She giggles and prods my shoulder with her finger. "You're old."

I look at Josh, feigning disapproval. "Thanks, jackass."

"Adrian! Language..."

I turn and see Janine hustling into the kitchen, dressed in her dark pink nurse's scrubs. She walks behind us, pausing to kiss Maria on the forehead.

"Just ignore Daddy, sweetie."

"Okay." says Maria as she shoves a fork-full of egg into her mouth.

Janine carries on into the kitchen, heading for the coffee and kissing Josh on the cheek as she passes. "Morning, sunshine."

"What's up, J?" he replies.

"Have a good time last night?"

He frowns. "What... ah... what d'you mean?"

She glances over her shoulder at him with a raised eyebrow. "Please. I can smell the perfume on you."

He immediately looks over at me apologetically.

I shake my head. "Dude, seriously? I thought you broke things off with her."

He shrugs. "I did, but she got all upset. Then we cracked open a bottle of wine. Then she wanted to go dancing..."

Janine walks back toward me, lightly slapping Josh's cheek as he passes him. "All right—my husband and daughter don't need to hear about your *dance classes*."

I put my hand up. "Hey, I could stand to hear about them..."

She clips me around the head as she passes me. "You do enough *dancing*."

Josh laughs. "My man!"

She sits down opposite me and casts an unimpressed glance at Josh, who holds a hand up in silent apology.

"Mmm-hmm. Anyway, what brings you here this early?" she asks him.

"Me and your lesser half have a meeting this morning, which..." He pauses to check his watch. "... we should really get going for, boss."

Janine looks at me. "Is this the new security thing you were talking about?"

I nod. "Yeah, our firm is trying to nail down a new long-term contract, and they need us to act as consultants for the potential client."

"Well, I hope it goes okay. Are you going to be home for dinner tonight?"

"I should be, but I'll let you know if anything changes." I stand and kiss Maria on the head. "Have a good day in school, monkey."

"Thanks, Daddy."

I move around the table and kiss Janine. "Hope your shift goes okay."

"See you tonight, soldier."

I look over at Josh. "You ready?"

He nods. "Always."

He follows me out of the house, down the short path, and onto the sidewalk. His car is parked outside the house across the street.

"You okay, man?" he asks as he unlocks the door.

"Yeah. Why wouldn't I be?"

We both get in and he guns the engine. It sounds like a

grenade exploding. A thin plume of dark smoke escapes through the exhaust.

As he pulls away from the curb, he says, "Because I know how much you hate lying to your family."

I sigh. "Yeah, I know. But it's for the best."

Both Josh and I left our respective armies at the same time. Officially, we both took an honorable discharge. But unbeknownst to almost everyone, including my wife and daughter, we *unofficially* left the army years ago. We worked for the same off-the-books CIA unit, known as D.E.A.D. We did a lot of things no one will admit to, but we did a lot of good for the world—I genuinely believe that.

However, times change, and budget cuts are a bitch. Because of 9/11, the country is doing a lot more to keep people safe than it used to. With so much emphasis on public security and transparency, there's little need for people to keep operating in the shadows like we did. That's why we both took our well-compensated leave when it was offered to us.

Having a healthy bank account is great, but after doing what we did for as long as we did, we were a little unsure what to do next. Our skill sets are... *specific*, shall we say, and don't lend themselves to your normal nine-to-five. When we first learned our time on Uncle Sam's black books was coming to an end, it was Josh who suggested I become a hitman. It pays well, it's flexible, and I've done very little besides kill people for the last thirteen years. I'm not saying it's perfect, but it's what I'm good at.

So, with Josh's help, we set up our own little enterprise almost six months ago. It's been going well. The work is steady, if a little slow at times. The payouts started off low, but my success rate, coupled with Josh's efforts at brand-building, as he calls it, has seen me quickly reach the stage where I can justify charging a higher rate. But it's still a competitive industry. You can't ask for too much because we're all bidding on the same contracts, and unless you have a very high reputation, contracts are typically won by the lowest bidder.

While we're both new to this business, neither of us are new to dealing with the kind of people this business attracts. Consequently, one of my conditions for doing this was that my family never finds out. I've never lied to Janine, but while I share most things with her, I'm smart enough to know that she doesn't need to know everything. My priority is keeping her and Maria safe, which means not telling her about the suspicious ten-year gap in my service record, or that I now kill people for money.

Hence all the talk of being security consultants. It's just easier to handle.

Josh turns right at a set of lights, putting the rising sun directly ahead of us. It's already warm, and I can't see it cooling down anytime soon. I pull the visor down to shield me from the glare. Josh has sunglasses on.

"So, this appointment..." I say. "Who's the client?"

"A guy named Perrelli," explains Josh. "Something of a big deal over in Brooklyn. Runs a lot of illegal businesses in the borough."

"Such as?"

He shrugs. "Money laundering, back-room poker, protection, extortion, drugs... you name it. Not much happens in that part of town without his knowledge."

"He sounds important. What does he need me for?"

"Well, apparently, a gang of Russians has moved into Brighton Beach and started their own criminal enterprise, which is bad for Perrelli's business. He wants them to stop."

"I assume he asked nicely and they refused?"

Josh nods. "Something like that. So, he's put a contract out on the gang's leader. Some guy who goes by the name Prizrak."

I frown. "What kind of a name's that?"

"It's an alias. A nickname which is apparently Russian for 'Ghost'."

I shake my head. "What kind of douchebag needs a nickname to impress anyone?"

Josh smiles. "The kind whose livelihood relies on scaring the shit out of horrible people."

"Whatever. So, my target is this... Prizrak guy?"

"Yeah. There's a file on the back seat for you."

I reach behind for it. It's a thin manila folder with a few sheets of paper inside.

Josh reaches across and taps the folder with his finger. "In there is everything I could find. Admittedly, it wasn't much. I've included a list of known associates. The problem we have with this guy is that no one knows where he operates from. Or, if they do, they aren't willing to admit it."

"I'm guessing I need to work my way through the list until I find him?"

"Looks like it, boss."

"How much is Perrelli paying us?"

"Seventy G's."

I glance over at him with wide eyes. "Seventy thousand? Holy shit, man!"

He laughs. "I know. Biggest payday to date. I'm telling you, bro, you're a natural at this."

I smile. "Not sure that's something to be proud of, but whatever works, right? Should be easy."

"Well, don't get too cocky. The Russians aren't known for being too forgiving of people who try to fuck with them. You should tread carefully."

I wave his concerns away. "I'll be fine. I don't suppose Perrelli's offering any help, is he?"

Josh shakes his head. "He's keeping as far away from this one as he can, in case there's any comeback."

I nod. "Understandable. But there won't be."

"Here's hoping, boss."

He navigates the increasingly busy traffic and turns onto I-95. It's just under two hours to Brooklyn from here. Plenty of time to plan the job.

2

We're parked across the street from a bakery on Neptune Avenue. The sidewalks are congested—far busier than the road. A diverse mix of people, all dressed for the summer, rush in every direction. We've been here maybe five minutes. I like to scope the place out and get a feel for it all —everything from the location of my target to the city I'm in and the people around me. I need to know as much as I can about the task ahead. It helps me anticipate every possible outcome. It helps me stay alive.

The bakery across the street is well-known to the locals for having the best fresh donuts in the city. What isn't common knowledge, however, is that an illegal gambling den belonging to my current employer, Mr. Perrelli, operates out of the basement. You can access it via the service alley running behind the bakery. He stated in his brief that he's recently begun attracting members of Prizrak's crew to their poker games. While there hasn't been any trouble yet, tensions are starting to brew between men on both sides, given Perrelli's open dislike of Prizrak's operation on his turf.

Sounds like the perfect place to start looking for information on my target's whereabouts.

"What are you thinking?" asks Josh, without taking his eyes off the bakery.

I shrug. "Figured I'd go in as a potential customer, engage whoever's there in some polite conversation, and see if I can find out anything useful without drawing any attention to myself."

He looks over at me with a deadpan expression. "Seriously?"

"Yeah, why not?"

He shifts in his seat to face me properly. "Oh, gee, I dunno. Let's think... Maybe because you have the people skills of sociopathic introvert and the patience of a child on Christmas morning who's been told to wait until the turkey's cooked before opening their presents."

I hold his gaze and raise an eyebrow. "A little harsh, don't you think?"

He shakes his head. "No. Honest, maybe."

"That's ridiculous. Name one time when I've failed to find out information without violence."

He sighs. "Saudi Arabia, back in '99. All you had to do was keep that guy talking while we made the extraction, but you knocked him out cold within two minutes, which brought his entire personal security team down on us. We had to shoot our way out of the restaurant."

"But that was—"

"Then there was Argentina in '01. You had to lay low in that village with Velasquez until we secured the intel, but what happened?"

I look away. "I blew up a building."

"You blew up a building. And then just last year, in Pakistan, we—"

"All right, I said name *one*. You've made your point."

"So, I'll ask you again. What's your plan?"

"Look, I know I'm not the best at being discreet..."

He scoffs. "No shit. At least you've learned the word, which is an improvement."

"Y'know, you don't need to be here..."

He smiles. "Please. You need someone to drive you away when this plan goes to shit."

"Kiss my ass, Josh."

I get out of the car and stretch, being careful not to let my sweater ride up too much and reveal my guns. I carry two Berettas with me when I'm working, holstered at my lower back, barrel-to-barrel in a T-shape. They're the M9 model. Lovely weapons. I'm still getting used to the weight, but Josh got his hands on this amazing harness for me. It's like a powerlifter's belt, which holds them in place and distributes the weight evenly, so having them on me doesn't restrict my movement.

I walk around the hood, nod a silent *see you later* to Josh, and jog across the street through a gap in the steady stream of traffic. The bakery is close to the corner, so I carry on walking past the storefront, glancing in as I do. It's busy, which is understandable this close to lunchtime. As I pass by the open door, I'm hit by the mouth-watering aroma of fresh bread and cake.

I could eat a dozen of those donuts right now...

Head in the game, Adrian. Head in the game.

I turn the corner, weave my way through the small crowd waiting to cross the street, and take the first left, heading along the alley that leads behind the bakery. It's narrow, made even more so by the large dumpsters that line the right-hand wall. As I make my way along, I notice almost every service door is open—all except one. The bakery's rear entrance is closed, and there's a guy in a suit standing beside it, looking as out of place as President Bush would at a science fair.

Gee, I wonder where the illegal gambling den is...

I approach the guy casually, trying to look as unassuming as possible. I slow and linger a few feet away from him until he notices me. After a moment, he acknowledges my presence by turning his head slightly toward me.

"What the fuck do you want?" he asks. His accent is classically Brooklyn-esque, where every word sounds aggressive, whether he intends them to be or not.

I nod a curt greeting. "Just looking to spend some cash, man. Heard this was the place..."

He shifts back to his rigid, detached position of staring straight ahead as if I'm not here.

"You heard wrong. Fuck off."

I take a long, deep breath, which doesn't fill me with as much patience as I intended. I can't stand bad manners or a bad attitude. It costs nothing to be polite. Besides, how does this place make any money with this prick standing guard outside, insulting potential customers?

I'll try again.

I step directly in front of him and flex my shoulders, naturally easing to my full height and width.

"Maybe I wasn't being clear before," I say. "We have the same boss, you and me. See, I'm an... independent contractor that Mr. Perrelli's brought in. Let's call me an auditor. I just wanna have a look inside and make sure he has the right level of security for his business."

The guy looks me up and down slowly. He's a little shorter than me, but a lot wider—mostly across the chest.

He looks as if he was poured into his suit. I'm guessing he does a lot of upper body work in the gym. He can probably bench three hundred, easy. He's probably no stranger to a fight, either. His nose looks as if it's accustomed to being broken.

Maybe not as familiar with *winning* fights...

"Bullshit. If that were true, someone would've told me."

I smile politely. "Yeah, I doubt that. Way I hear it, associates of one of Mr. Perrelli's business rivals have been seen here. That can't be good for the image, surely? And if it's your job to decide who goes in or out of the... *bakery*... then any issues your boss is facing are likely down to your outstanding lack of competence."

His brow furrows into an expression laced with anger and bad intentions. I kind of figured it would, although I have no wish to start something with anyone who's supposed to be on my side. That said, I see his legs and arms tensing, which means he's preparing to do something silly, like attack me.

I just want to get inside and see who there is to talk to. Places like this, in my experience, aren't affected by the time of day. But first...

This guy starts to move forward. He transfers his weight onto his front foot, preparing to launch a big, heavy haymaker at my head. I cut him off by lunging elbow-first into him. The thick, dense part of my forearm, close to where the arm bends to form the point of the elbow, connects with his chest, a couple of inches below his throat. On impact, I lean into him, pressing my elbow hard against him, as if I'm trying to push the wall behind him through. I pin him against the closed door, allowing all the energy and momentum to transfer from me to him.

I smell the nicotine on his breath as the air rushes from him.

Holding him in place, I bring my left hand up and over, delivering a sharp, jabbing hook to the side of his jaw.

Consciousness leaves him almost as fast as his breath did.

I grimace to myself as I hear Josh's voice inside my head repeatedly chanting *I told you so*.

"Shit."

Feeling the lights go out, I quickly bring both hands under his arms and guide him over to the chair resting to the side of the door.

Christ, he's heavy!

"There we go, big guy. Just relax. Sit down and take the weight off." I position him in the seat and rest him upright against the back. "Don't worry about it, man. It happens to the best of us. Well, most of us. Well... you. This shit happens to people like you. You see, *I'm* a winner."

I slowly move away from him, making sure he isn't going to fall over, and open the door.

Right... let's see who wants to talk to me.

3

The door opens into a small vestibule. A corridor stretches out before me, with an open door at the far end, revealing the back rooms of the bakery. There's also a metal staircase set back on the right, which presumably descends to the basement.

I think I know which way I need to go...

I close the door gently behind me and head down the stairs. What little light there was by the door fades away. Darkness closes in, wrapping itself around me like a blanket. My footsteps echo on the metal steps. After a few moments of being unable to see my hand in front of my face, a faint glow of light appears below me. Another few moments and I'm bathed in fluorescence.

The basement area consists of two rooms—the one the stairs lead into and another adjoined to it, which is only accessible through another door in the corner. I assume the party's in there. This room is mostly empty. The walls are lined with rusted shelving, filled with boxes of all sizes. The buzz from the overhead lights is giving me a headache already.

There's another guy standing beside the final door ahead of me. He's dressed the same as his friend outside. He's a little more conscious though.

For now.

I walk toward him, instinctively tugging my sweater down to make sure my weapons are concealed.

"Help you?" he asks.

I'll try my story again.

I nod. "Yeah, I'm here to give Mr. Perrelli some of my hard-earned cash."

One corner of his mouth curls slightly. He gestures to the door with his thumb—a silent invitation. He doesn't move to open it. As I reach for the handle, I feel his hand grip my shoulder. It's firm but not aggressive.

I look first at his hand, then at him. "Problem?"

"Gotta search you, man."

Shit.

I don't know why I hoped he wouldn't want to search me. It stands to reason that he would. It's his job. The problem is, I'm almost out of the patience needed to keep being all diplomatic and discreet. And I can't exactly start explaining the actual reason I'm here—the whole point of Perrelli hiring me was to stop anyone finding out Prizrak's pending demise has anything to do with him.

What to do... what to do...

See, on one hand, this would go a lot smoother if I had some of Perrelli's men helping me. Or even just letting me get on with my job.

But on the other hand, it's a lot easier to get information out of people when you're holding a gun, and this guy won't let me go in there armed, regardless of how helpful he thinks he's being.

I hear Josh's voice in my head again.

Whatever.

"Let me save you the hassle, pal," I say to the guard. "I have two Berettas at my back, neither of which I'm giving to you. I'm here looking for someone. I don't want any trouble, but I won't let you stop me, either."

The guy retracts his hand and holds my gaze. I think he might be realizing how I got past his friend upstairs. I watch his body make miniscule movements in all directions— twitches of indecision.

Smart man.

"Who are you looking for?" he asks.

"A guy named Prizrak. You know him?"

He shifts on the spot and avoids my gaze.

That's a *yes*.

"Look, I know he isn't here," I continue. "But the way I hear it, some of his associates might be. I want to ask them where I can find him. Nice and polite."

He remains hesitant. His hand restlessly hovers near his jacket.

I shrug. "Or I can break this door down using your face and cause a whole world of shit for anyone in there. It's up to you."

He's not happy. I can tell. He's got the clenched jaw. The stiff body. The furrowed brow.

But...

He sighs, accepting defeat.

"There's... ah... there's six guys playing in total. Four employees. Just..." He winces at his own resignation. "Who are you again?"

I smile. "I'm the guy who took out the doorman upstairs.

I'm the guy with two guns at my back. And, if you'd be kind enough to indulge me, I'm the guy who was never here. We understand one another?"

With a silent, visible curse to himself, he nods and opens the door.

"Thank you."

I step inside.

Finally, I'm getting somewhere.

4

Well, I don't mind admitting, I wasn't expecting *this*.

It feels like I've just stepped inside a closet and stepped out into Narnia. Compared to the room behind me, this place is Vegas! The walls are lined with red, velvet padding —which I'm guessing acts as soundproofing, as there's background music playing that I couldn't hear when the door was closed. The carpet is thick underfoot. There are five separate tables, all dark wood and well-maintained, offering a variety of casino-style entertainment. Let's see... we've got blackjack, roulette, poker, craps, and...

Hmm.

The fifth table, in the far corner, is set away from the rest of the room. From here, it looks like another poker table, but judging by the serious expressions worn by the two men sitting at it, I'm guessing that's the big money game.

There are two more guys playing blackjack. A pretty, young blonde woman is dealing to them, wearing the hell out of a fitted trouser suit. There's a portly gentleman hunched over the roulette wheel, cradling a glass of what looks like scotch as if it were his own child. Finally, there's a guy in a bad suit shooting dice on the craps table. The nearest poker table is empty. There's also a modest but surprisingly well-stocked bar in the far-left corner, ahead of me. There's a bartender standing behind it, staring into space as he polishes a glass.

No one's looked up at me. I guess there's little need for curiosity in a place like this. If you're gambling in an illegal casino run by a local gangster, you could be forgiven for assuming everyone who walks in here has been vetted by the security guard and is in no way a threat.

I mean, who would be stupid enough to walk into a back-alley casino and start shit, right?

I make my way over to the bartender. He looks bored. Plus, the nature of his job means he'll likely talk to almost everyone who passes through, so he's a good place to start asking questions.

I sit on one of the high-back stools and lean an arm on the bar. He looks across and nods a polite, non-committal greeting. I return the gesture.

"What are you having, buddy?" he asks.

His dark hair is greased back against his head. He flashes a practiced, salesman's smile.

I bet he lives off the tips in this place.

I glance behind him at the bar. "Just a beer. Thanks."

He nods and turns to get it for me. No judgment. Why should he care that it's barely lunchtime? This place most likely runs twenty-four-seven. People who spend their money here will drink accordingly.

He places the bottle down in front of me and flips the

cap off with an opener attached to his belt by a retractable cord.

"Enjoy."

I nod. "Thanks."

The bottle's cold and damp in my hand. I take a long gulp.

Man, that's refreshing.

"You here to try to your luck?" he asks.

I shrug. "Maybe. Haven't decided yet."

He flicks an eyebrow up. "This ain't the kinda place people usually come if they're undecided."

I take another gulp of my beer and smile. "Yeah, so I hear. So, do you, ah... do you get to know many people who come in here?"

He shrugs modestly. "As much as a guy like me can, y'know? It's my job to make customers feel welcome and keep them drinking. Not everyone cares for the conversation, but most are polite enough—even if they're only polite because they're afraid of the repercussions, y'know what I mean?"

He grins, almost proudly.

"I take it Mr. Perrelli doesn't take too kindly to trouble in here," I reply.

The grin fades a little.

"Yeah. He likes the place to remain respectful, y'know? In this line of work, you live and die by your reputation."

I nod in agreement. "I get that. Have you seen any trouble in here recently?"

He looks around for a moment. At first, I thought it was hesitation. I figured I'd pushed too soon. But then I realized it was for effect. He's the kind of guy who loves to talk.

"Last couple of weeks, a few fellas have been coming in here that Mr. Perrelli ain't taken too kindly to," he offers.

Bingo.

I raise my eyebrow slightly. "Any reason?"

He leans forward, his eyes darting in all directions.

"Don't get me wrong," he says, lowering his voice. "It ain't like they were causing any real trouble. And their money was good, y'know? But they were... how can I say? They were loud. Maybe a little crass. Like they thought being here was their way of taking a shot at the establishment."

"Or the guy running it..."

"Exactly, man."

I look around too, feigning interest. "So, who were they? These guys..."

"I don't know. They didn't talk much to me. But word is they're on the payroll of a new player in town. I heard a couple of the security guys talking."

I shrug. "So, why let them in, if they're causing problems?"

"It's like I said, man. It's all about the reputation. If word gets around that Mr. Perrelli's turning customers with good money away for no reason, he'd be finished within a week."

"But he had good reason..."

"He doesn't. Not really. Sure, reading between the lines, maybe there's more to it, but bottom line is they weren't any louder than anyone else in here when they're gambling and drinking."

I take another gulp of beer. "Hmm. Sounds to me like these guys knew just what buttons to push and how long to push 'em for."

"I hear that, buddy." He straightens up. "But 'theirs not to reason why', am I right?"

I tilt the neck of my bottle toward him in silent cheers.

"'Theirs but to do and die'," I add.

We laugh lightly together.

This is going well. You can always rely on bartenders or waitresses to talk when you need answers. I think I'll try my luck a little.

"So, buddy, I'm gonna be here a while. Reckon you could point these guys out to me, should they come in? Just so I know who to avoid socializing with, y'know?"

"Sure thing, man." He nods behind me, toward the poker table in the opposite corner. "Two of them are in the high-stakes game right now."

I casually glance over my shoulder to get a better look at them. I couldn't make out their features from the door, but from the bar, I can see their faces more clearly.

I turn back to face the bartender and smile. "Aces."

5

I order another beer, nod a polite farewell to my new friend, and walk casually toward the poker table in the far corner. I haven't been in many casinos, but from what I recall, it's common for people to hover near tables they're thinking about sitting at, to get a feel for the game and the competition before committing their money.

I'm maybe ten feet away now, doing my best to look awkward and uncertain while assessing the threat level of the guys playing cards.

They're both similar in build, at least from the waist up. One is clean-shaven; the other has three-day-old stubble. Both have short, dark hair and the kind of complexion that makes you assume they're European—the defined, pale features and eyes that glow with a deceptive strength. They're sitting slightly apart, at the dealer's ten and two, respectively. One has a significantly larger stack of chips than the other.

In my head, I'm running through all the different ways I could play this. It's something I used to do with my D.E.A.D. unit. It drove Josh fucking nuts. I've always had this thing about being prepared. If you ignore the inevitable insults that center around boy scouts, it's easy to see why it's the only way to approach things.

Take now, for example. I could do exactly what I just did with the bartender—sit down, engage them, build up some rapport, and maybe get scraps of information from them. It's civil but long-winded and unlikely to get me what I need. These guys work for a Russian gangster, so you have to assume they have the *hired douchebag* attitude of someone who thinks they're tougher than they are because of who they hang with. My approach is unlikely to yield the same results as I got earlier. The chances are these two will ultimately try to attack me, so that rules out that plan.

Alternatively, I could walk over there, quickly smash one guy's head into the table and place the barrel of my gun against the other. The surprise would remove any chance of retaliation. Plus, having a gun to someone's head usually serves as a good incentive to start answering questions. The problem with that is I would be causing a scene in front of witnesses. I know no one's going to call the cops, but it would draw attention to me, likely resulting in word getting back to my target that two of his boys were fucked up in one of Perrelli's establishments, which wouldn't end well for anyone. So, that's not an option either.

I think my only viable play is to make them attack me, then use my self-defense as a way of getting physical enough to ask them questions without it looking like anyone's truly to blame. That way, everyone's reputation stays intact, and I'm just some asshole who got into a fight and earned himself a lifetime ban from this place, which is fine with me.

Here we go.

I walk heavy-footed toward the table and slam my bottle down on it as I take a seat. I chuckle randomly as I reach for my wallet and throw two hundred bucks on the table.

"Deal me in, champ," I say to the dealer.

He casts a disapproving eye over me and glances apologetically to the other two.

"Sir, the low blind is currently one hundred and fifty dollars," he explains professionally. "That stake will only buy you one hand."

"Whatever, man." I shrug and laugh, then look over at Prizrak's boys. "Can you believe this guy?"

The men exchange a glance but say nothing.

I look at the dealer again. "I'm feeling lucky, man. Hit me."

He takes a short breath. "Very well, sir. The game is No Limits Texas Hold 'Em."

He exchanges my cash for chips and deals us all two cards, face-down. I take a quick look at mine. Pair of sixes. Not bad. I glance up at the others, trying to get a read on them. The guy farthest away, with next-to-no chips in front of him, is holding his own cards close to his chest. I watch his expression. There's not much to go on, but I do see the faintest of quivers in one corner of his mouth.

I'm guessing he has a decent pair of cards.

I turn my attention to the other guy, sitting to my right. Looking at his chips, I reckon he's up maybe fifteen hundred bucks. He's checked his cards and committed them to memory, so he has no need to hold them. He's expressionless. I examine his eyes for any hint of a tell, but there's nothing. You would think he was in a coma.

I can see why he's winning.

A little luck here would be great, but it's not essential.

We all place our bets. I go all-in, naturally. The community cards are dealt in turn, and more bets are placed between the two guys.

"Call it," says the guy with no chips. He turns his cards over. "Two pairs, *suka!*"

I don't speak many languages. In fact, based on fluency, I barely speak one. But I have a high school level of understanding in a bunch of others. And by that, I mean I know the insults in about fifteen dialects. I'm pretty sure *suka* is 'bitch' in Russian.

The guy with all the money smiles as he theatrically turns his cards over. "Three eights."

He's still chuckling as he reaches for the pot, which is around four hundred dollars.

I slam my hand on the table. "Not so fast, comrade." I turn my cards over and grin. "Full house. Sixes over eights. How d'you like me now, shit-stains?"

I drag the pot over to me ceremoniously and start counting my chips loudly.

"Fifty... one-hundred... one-fifty..." I pause to look at them. They don't look happy. "What's the matter, boys? Surely, you should be used to losing to an American by now?"

Holy shit, that did it!

They both just sprang to their feet as if their chairs were on fire, sending both of their respective seats flying backward. The one now standing farthest from me slams his fist on the table and yells something I don't understand, but I assume it isn't a compliment. The other takes a step toward me and points his finger in my face.

"I don't know who the fuck you think you are, asshole, but you should learn some fucking respect."

My gaze is drawn to his finger. It's literally inches from

my face, and he's jabbing the air to put extra emphasis on his words.

I hate when people do that—when they get right up in my business and invade my personal space. There's no need for it. You can threaten someone just fine from a couple of feet away, y'know?

I feel a burning in my chest as the anger and frustration within starts to rise.

I just need to keep my cool a few minutes longer...

"Hey, take it easy now, fellas," I say. "How about I use my winnings to buy us all a round of drinks? What do you say?"

He presses his finger into my chest, just below my left shoulder.

"I say fuck you. Give me my money back, and maybe we won't shoot you."

I let out a loud sigh.

Why did he have to go and put his finger on me? It was all going so well...

I grab his finger and quickly break it. The pop is audible, but the guy's screams soon drown it out. I use the broken finger for leverage and force him to his knees. As he reaches the right height, I deliver a knee, swift and precise, into his face. I feel the cartilage in his nose cave under the impact. He falls backward, his good hand unsure which injury to cradle.

The second he hits the deck, one of my Berettas is in my hand, aimed unwaveringly at the other Russian.

"Don't do anything stupid, like your friend here," I say to him. I glance around the room. Everyone's frozen to the spot, staring at me. I smile apologetically. "Nothing to see here, folks. This is... ah... this is self-defense."

The guy on the floor yells out in pain. "Fuck you, asshole!"

I roll my eyes before taking a step to the side of him and bringing the sole of my boot down hard on his face. His head rolls limply to the side.

"Quiet now, junior. The grown-ups are talking." I look at his friend. "Listen, I ain't here to cause trouble, but I have questions that need answering, and I'm hoping you're my guy. Are you my guy?"

His gaze switches rapidly between my face and the barrel of my gun, which is still aimed between his eyes.

He nods. "W-what do you want to know?"

I smile. "Atta boy. You work for a man who calls himself Prizrak, correct?"

Another hurried nod of the head.

"I want to meet him. Where is he?"

He goes to speak but visibly hesitates, as if he's choking on the words.

"W-w-why?" he asks.

"I have some business to discuss with him."

"H-he will kill you."

It's not difficult to hear the fear in his voice.

"Let me worry about that. Just tell me where he is."

He shakes his head in short, snappy movements. "I can't! He'll... he'll kill me if I tell you!"

I gesture to my gun with a gentle nod. "What do you think I'm gonna do if you *don't* tell me? Take you out for a steak dinner?"

Whoever this Prizrak prick is, he's put the fear of God in the people who work for him.

This guy...

Oh my God, seriously?

The guy's started crying.

I roll my eyes. "Get a grip, man. Jesus! Have a little respect for yourself."

He kneels in front of the poker table and hangs his head. "I don't w-want to die!"

"Then tell me where I can find your boss, and you won't have to."

He looks up at me, exasperated. His eyes are wide and bloodshot. "If I talk to you, he will kill me!"

I shake my head. "If you tell me where he is, I'll put a bullet between his eyes, so he won't be able to."

The guy's jaw hangs loose.

I shrug. "I'm just being honest. If you tell me, I'll kill him and not you. You have my word on that."

He looks across at his friend, still lying unconscious next to me. Then he looks around at all the people watching. Finally, his gaze rests on me.

He takes a deep breath. "There's a warehouse on the boardwalk, close to the pier. That's where the operation runs out of."

I flick the safety on and re-holster the Beretta, tugging my sweater down to cover it.

"See, that wasn't so hard, was it?" I turn on my heels and head for the door. As I pass the bar, I glance over at the bartender and nod. "Tell Mr. Perrelli I'm sorry for the disruption. Won't happen again."

He confirms with a disbelieving nod.

I walk out, smile courteously to the security guard in the other room, and head up the stairs. I wonder if the guy I left outside is still out cold?

6

Josh is just finishing his burger. I finished mine a couple of minutes ago. We're standing side-by-side, leaning against the hood of the car, enjoying the sun and the sea breeze. We parked on the street, one over from Prizrak's warehouse, facing the ocean and the beach.

"Do you think Perrelli will be pissed at you?" asks Josh.

I shake my head. "Nah. There was no real harm done. No damage to the place. And the client I beat up was one of Prizrak's men, so he won't lose any sleep over that. None of this is on him. I made a point of being the stranger in town, y'know?"

Josh nods. "Which is all well and good, except you told one of them you intend to kill this Prizrak guy. What possessed you, Adrian?"

I shrug. "It was a calculated risk. You should've seen it, man. That guy was terrified. I needed to remove that fear to get him talking, so I said what I had to. Bottom line, it worked."

"Yeah, it did. But for all you know, the moment you walked out of that casino, your new friend could have picked up the phone and warned his boss you were coming."

"He could've done, yeah, but I doubt it. He saw what I did to his friend. He wouldn't have risked it. I reckon he was low-level. Happy to be involved. Happy to play gangster. But he wasn't looking to be in any real danger. Sure, he was scared of his boss, but he was thinking short-term, and back there, he was more scared of me."

Josh smiles, mostly to himself. "You've got it all pegged, haven't you?"

"What do you mean?"

"This business. You think you have it all figured out."

I shrug. "What's there to figure out? We spent the last decade secretly fighting terrorists to protect this country. Compared to what we've been through... what we've done... some wannabe Tony Montana with a fancy nickname is unlikely to give me anything to think about. It's simple, Josh. We find the target. I kill him. Nothing else to worry about."

"I hear you, boss, I do. And you're a natural at this. With you planning and executing the hits, and me finding the jobs and marketing you, we're unstoppable. But don't get ahead of yourself. You have a habit sometimes of seeing things too black-and-white. The world's grayer than you'd think. Just because this Prizrak guy isn't a terrorist in some mountain hideout doesn't mean he isn't dangerous."

"I know, man. Relax. You worry too much."

"And you don't worry enough."

I push away from the car and stretch before looking

back at him with a smile. "You're the Yin to my Yang, brother."

Josh shakes his head. "And you're the ass to the hole."

I laugh as he climbs back in the car and guns the engine. He turns in the street and disappears in a cloud of exhaust fumes. I head across the street to the boardwalk.

After leaving the casino, Josh did some research on the location using his new laptop. He loves his gadgets and insisted on getting a top-of-the-line portable computer to have with him on the road. It cost a small fortune, and while I don't pretend to understand how it works, I must admit the man's worked minor miracles with it since we started doing this.

There was very little history on the building Prizrak's guy gave up. It was bought by a shell company about eight months ago and paid for in cash, so there's no paper trail.

There are no security cameras on this strip of boardwalk, so I'm scouting the place while Josh tries to find more information on my target. That idiot in the casino said this is where the main operation is based, so I'm hoping for some regular traffic in and out of here. With a bit of luck, I might even get eyes on the man himself.

I sit on a bench, my back to the water, and watch the world go by, waiting for any sign of my target.

7

That didn't take as long as I thought it would. A black sedan with one of those stupid-looking spoilers stuck to the trunk just parked outside the warehouse, in one of the three spaces beside the large roller doors.

Four doors open. Four men appear.

Three of them are carbon copies of each other. Thin sweaters beneath sleeveless bodywarmers—oblivious to the time of year. Faded jeans. Combat boots. The driver has a gun tucked in his waistband at the back. The two who climbed out of the back have matching SMG's. From where I'm sitting, they look like Heckler and Koch UMP45s, but I could be wrong—I'm probably fifty feet away right now.

The fourth guy was riding shotgun. He's tall, with a thick beard and no obvious weapon. He's wearing a business suit without a tie. I recognize him from the grainy photo in Josh's file. It was a side profile shot from a distance, black and white, but there's no question.

Mr. Prizrak, I presume.

He's talking to the other three. It looks like he's giving instructions, with lots of hand gestures. He keeps looking around, up and down the boardwalk too, as if he's waiting for someone. I'm far enough away that I'm not worried he'll see me—not that he'll think twice, even if he did—so I keep watching. The two guys with SMGs disappear inside the warehouse, through a service door next to the rollers. The driver stands with Prizrak, scanning the area like a body-guard would for his detail.

What are they waiting for?

...

...

...

That, I'm guessing.

A truck's approaching from the right, no bigger than a transit. It drives past the lot and reverses, putting the rear doors flush against the warehouse rollers. The driver climbs out of the cab and walks around the hood to speak with Prizrak.

There's maybe thirty seconds of conversation before the three of them head inside.

Hmmm.

I wonder what's in the truck?

Should I go look?

No, that would be crazy.

But...

What do we know?

Not fucking much is the answer to that.

Perrelli's intel and Josh's research found very little on Prizrak or his operation. Regardless of how ridiculous he sounds using a nickname, it's certainly appropriate. The guy is a ghost.

If I walk away now, there's no guarantee he'll be back here anytime soon.

On the other hand, right now, I know exactly where my target is. Sure, there are four other guys with him—three of whom I know for certain are armed—but still, it's nothing I can't handle. Maybe. Plus, at the very least, peeking inside might give me insight into his behavior or his business interests. That could prove invaluable if I need to track him down again.

I can't believe I'm still sitting here when we all know I'm going to sneak into that warehouse.

I cross the street and head down the alley that runs along the opposite side of the warehouse to the roller doors. There's got to be another way in.

...

...

...

Bingo.

A rusty fire escape is loosely attached to the end of the building, just around the corner, halfway along the alley. I climb it carefully, as quickly as I dare. I don't want to make any noise, obviously, but I'm more worried this thing will fall off the goddamn wall, it's that old!

At the top is a wooden door with small, broken windows. I reach inside and try the handle. It's locked, but it feels very loose in the frame. If I'm careful, I might be able to...

CRACK!

...force it open.

Shit, that was loud.

I sit tight for a couple of minutes to make sure no one heard me.

...

...

...

I think I'm good.

Crouching, I move inside. The door leads onto a metal gantry that runs around all sides of the interior. There's a foreman's office straight ahead of me. Stairs leading down to the floor are in the opposite corner.

I creep forward and make my way left, away from the office. I peer over the railing. It's empty down there. A few wooden crates are stacked against the right wall. The rollers are up, and I see the rear doors of the van stood open, although I can't see inside it. There's no sign of life below, but I hear movement and muffled conversation from somewhere. They might be beneath where I'm standing.

I continue moving around, taking each step with more care than I have patience for, so they won't know I'm here. I follow the gantry to the right, heading for the stairs. I feel the breeze coming in through the open doors.

I edge along another few feet and stop. From here, I see the part of the warehouse that was below me when I first came in. The three guys who arrived with Prizrak are standing in a line, facing right. I can only see a pair of shoes and a leg in front of them. I'm guessing that's the man himself. No sign of the driver.

What's that in the corner, on the other side of them? It looks like a room. No, wait. It's a cage, or a cell. Two sides of it are wooden, attached to the warehouse walls. The other two sides are bars. I can't see what's inside because the armed assholes are in the way.

This might work. They're standing maybe forty feet from me. I could take out one of them from here, definitely. Maybe two, if I'm lucky and they're not organized. I have the high ground, which is advantageous. Plus, I didn't see a door around the back of this place, which means the only way in or out is through the metal roller doors and the service entrance, or the fire escape, which I'm blocking. If they try to leave, I have a clear shot.

But I don't know where the driver is, and I don't know if he's armed. That's a big variable. And I don't know if Prizrak is armed. It didn't look like it outside, but I don't know how big his operation is. There might be another fifty guys just a phone call away...

Am I being too impetuous here? Am I rushing for the sake of it? Maybe Josh was right. Maybe I *am* a little impulsive. But there's nothing wrong with having confidence in your own ability to—

What... the... fuck...

The guys below me have moved.

I can see inside the cage.

There are five young girls huddled together in the corner. And I mean *young*. One of them doesn't look any older than Maria.

What kind of operation is Prizrak running?

8

This isn't right. This is just... this isn't right. I know my job is simply to take out Prizrak, but...

I shake my head, trying to dislodge the image of those kids, but I can't take my eyes off them, so it's pointless.

This isn't right.

I'm high enough that I shouldn't be spotted in people's peripheral vision, so I make my way farther along the gantry, toward the corner where the stairs are. The men are hanging around near the door. From this vantage point, I have a clearer view of Prizrak. He's talking to the driver.

He hands him an envelope. They shake hands. The driver is heading toward me—toward the doors. It looks like he's leaving.

I'll have to let him go. I don't want to, but he's not the priority here. The three assholes with guns are still below me, their backs to the warehouse floor, staring out past the truck.

The driver moves out of my line of sight. I inch along until I reach the top of the stairs. There's still no indication that anyone's seen me.

Good.

I grip the handrail and look down, where Prizrak is, but my gaze keeps getting drawn to the cage in the corner.

Those poor girls. They're all wearing clothes that are too big for them. Their faces are dirty. I wonder if they've been brought over from another country? I feel myself shudder as I think of all the possible reasons they would be here.

I look at the smallest one. I reckon she's the youngest. Maria's face appears in my mind. Her beautiful smile. Her infectious laugh. She has her mother's eyes. I take a breath. It's as if I can feel her hand holding mine. She's my everything.

And now I re-focus on the smallest girl in that cage. All I can think is that somewhere in the world, right now, is a man doing the same thing I just did. A father, thinking about his daughter. He's probably staring at a wall, nursing a glass of liquor, crying as he tries to make sense of the fact his baby girl was taken from him.

That could be me. That girl down there... she could be Maria.

This ain't right.

I can't just leave them there.

Fuck Perrelli. He can keep his money. I owe it to the five fathers who are missing their little girls right now to put a stop to... whatever *this* is. To stop Prizrak, so he can't destroy any more families. Any more lives.

I hear the truck drive away outside.

Fuck it.

I sprint down the stairs. The three guys with guns are

lined up right in front of me. I don't break stride. I don't hesitate. I run straight at them. I shoulder charge the first guy, who goes flying into the other two. They were unprepared, and I send all three flying across the floor.

In a split-second, I have a Beretta in my hand. I turn and aim it at Prizrak, who's standing on the opposite side of the warehouse. He's rooted to the spot, transfixed on me. I fire once. The bullet hits his shoulder and punches him to the floor.

I spin around. The men are scrambling to their feet. The two with SMGs have them on a strap, so they're still hanging around their necks. The other guy lost his gun when he fell.

It doesn't matter.

I fire three more shots in quick succession, each one aimed at the head of a guy in front of me.

They all find their target. They all crumple to the floor, each one seconds apart. A large, dark stain expands beneath their bodies.

The adrenaline is pumping like crazy. My heart's about to beat out of my chest. But the anger... Holy shit! I don't ever remember feeling this angry in my life. I've seen and done some wicked shit in my time, but there's never been any emotion in it. I've never taken it home with me. But this... this is going to be with me forever, and I can't handle that. My brain isn't built to fathom what's going on here. I don't understand—and I don't want to.

I stride quickly across the warehouse, toward Prizrak. He's managed to get up on one knee. He has a hand clamped to his shoulder, stained with the blood from his wound.

I stop a few feet from him.

He looks up at me. "Who... who are you?"

"I'm like you," I reply. "I'm a ghost."

I smash the butt of my gun into his temple, and he crashes to the floor.

I dash over to the cage and open it. The girls scream.

I put my gun away and hold my hands up, palms facing forward.

"Hey, hey, it's okay. I'm not going to hurt you, I promise."

They all exchange looks of confusion and fear. After a moment, the tallest girl pushes to the front of the group, putting the rest of them behind her.

"W-who... are... you?" she asks.

Her English is broken. I can't place the accent. It's possibly Romanian.

"I'm here to kill him." I point behind me to Prizrak's body. "You're all free now. Do you understand? You can go."

The girl frowns. Her eyes are bloodshot, her face gaunt. "Free? We can... leave?"

I nod and smile. "Yes. There is a police station not far from here. Do you understand police?"

The girl nods silently.

"Good. Head outside and turn left. Then take your next left and keep going until you see the police station. Tell them everything. They'll look after you."

She nods again and turns to face the group. She speaks quickly. I don't understand what she's saying, but I can guess. One by one, they file out of the cage and run for the door. The last girl out is the small one, who reminds me of my own daughter. She pauses in front of me and smiles. It's a child's smile, full of innocence and hope.

I feel so sorry for each one of them that their lives have led them here.

She runs off to join the others, giving the three corpses a wide berth as she disappears outside.

I turn and look down at Prizrak's unconscious body. "You won't like this next part. I can promise you that, you sick bastard."

9

It's amazing what you can find lying around an old warehouse.

A decent length of rope. A knife. A can half-full of gasoline. A pack of cigarettes. And a lighter.

Perrelli wanted Prizrak dead to send a message to anyone else thinking of setting up business on his turf, so they knew it wasn't a good idea.

This is going to be one hell of a loud message.

It's taken me a good half hour, but it's been worth it. First, I closed the roller doors, so the whole world couldn't see what I was doing. Then I dragged the dead guys over to where Prizrak is and stacked them against each other. Next, I stripped Prizrak naked and tied the rope around his ankles. I went back up onto the gantry and hoisted him up, tying it off on the railing. He's currently hanging upside-down, naked, maybe three feet above a pile of his dead henchmen.

I needed a few minutes to catch my breath, but I'm good now.

I slap his face.

"Huh? W-what? What's happening?"

He blinks slowly. I imagine there's a little fog after being knocked out cold. He frowns, probably against the headache, as he tries to figure out what's happened and where he is. His thought process is displayed on his face.

I crouch in front of him. His eyeline is maybe six inches above mine. I fix him with a hard stare. My jaw aches from tensing against the rage I can barely control.

"What's happening is the very least you deserve, you twisted fuck." I lunge forward and punch him hard in the face. "Mr. Perrelli says 'hello', by the way."

He spits blood out and laughs. "Perrelli? That fucking coward. I knew he didn't have the balls to come at me himself. You must be his hired dog..."

I pace away from him. "See, even on a normal day, trash-talking and mind games don't work on me. I'm the undis-puted king when it comes to running your mouth, trust me. But today... today isn't a normal day. Today, I don't mind admitting I'm so blinded by a level of fury I never knew existed, nothing you say even registers. So, save it."

"I will find you, dog."

Can you believe this guy is smiling? He's got some balls, I'll give him that.

Speaking of which...

I take my Beretta out and aim it at his groin.

His eyes go wide. "No! Wait! Hold on! I'll pay you anything you want, just... please, no!"

Amazing.

"Tell me what you were doing with those girls," I say to him.

He looks over at the cage, confused.

"Oh, I let them go. They're probably sitting in a police station by now, telling some desk sergeant the horror story that is their lives. Thanks to you. I'll ask you again. What were you doing with those girls?"

His breathing is short and rapid. No doubt, he's panicking at the fact he's naked, and a gun is pointing at his cock.

"I... I brought them into the country on a private boat... from Serbia."

"Why?"

"For... for auction."

"What?"

He sighs. "The internet... it is an amazing thing. You can buy anything on there, if you know where to look."

I shake my head with disbelief. "You were selling these girls on the internet?"

"I have buyers all over the world. They usually go for a hundred grand *each*."

I pace away again. I can't comprehend what he's saying. How is this possible? Never mind the technicalities; how could anyone even *think* of doing something like that in the first place?

I face him and point my gun at his junk again.

"I want you to know something," I say. "I've been a soldier since I was a kid. I was eighteen years old in basic training. I was part of Desert Shield. I saw terrible things done by terrible people. I worked for years doing the government's dirty work for more money than you can imagine. I've been to every kind of hellhole this planet has to offer. I've killed a lot of bad people. And then I retired and became a hitman. A gun for hire. And d'you know what? I'm pretty good at it. I'm a goddamn expert at erasing people. I've taken out drug dealers, abusive husbands, stock brokers... you name it. I've seen it all. I've done it all. But here's the kicker..." I crouch in front of him again and stare into his eyes. "Even after everything I've experienced in my life, I have *never* met someone as depraved as you. You are the absolute worst piece of shit I have ever encountered. And you'll be dealt with accordingly."

I stand and move over to a large crate I've been using as a table.

Prizrak tries to look at me but can't spin himself around.

"What are you doing? Where are you going?"

I move back in front of him, holding the can of gasoline.

His eyes meet mine. I see the fear on his face.

"P-please, no! God, no! I'll do anything. I'll pay you anything!"

I shake my head. "This isn't about money. Now pay attention to this next part. I'll say it slowly, so you understand. There is nothing you can say or do to change what is about to happen to you. You are about to die in the most horrific way I can imagine. And given what I've just told you about my life, I'm sure you can appreciate that my imagination is pretty fucking vivid."

I splash the gasoline all over his body, soaking him completely. I then drain it over the pile of dead bodies beneath him and walk away, leaving a small trail behind me, all the way to the middle of the warehouse floor.

He coughs and sputters and spits.

"God, no! Please!"

I ignore him. There's nothing more to say. I walk past him to the crate. I put the empty can down and pick up the cigarettes and lighter, which I shove in my pocket for now.

Then I pick up the knife. It's a rusted machete. God

knows what it's doing in here. It's still sharp though, which is what matters.

I stand in front of him. He's still screaming and begging. I try to think of something to say. Something final, to hammer the point home that he's a sick bastard who deserves what's about to happen. But I realize there's no need.

I take a deep breath.

I move the knife quickly, swiping left to right, and slice clean through his manhood. Everything that once lived between his legs rolls down his body and drops onto the three corpses beneath him. Blood erupts from the wound. His screams are filled with genuine agony.

"That's for those young girls you were about to sell," I say.

I drop to a crouch and swipe the blade again, this time across his throat. I keep it shallow enough that he won't bleed out too quickly, but it's deep enough to stop his screaming. More blood spews from him like a geyser, covering his face in deep crimson. His eyes are wide, glowing white against the red mask.

"That's for Perrelli.'

I stand and bury the blade deep into his sternum, a couple of inches above his naval.

"And *that* was for me. I hope you burn in hell for what you did."

I walk into the middle of the warehouse floor and take out the cigarette and lighter. Behind me, I hear the desperate gurgles as Prizrak tries to breathe. As things stand, I'd give him twenty seconds before he bleeds out.

I place a cigarette between my lips and light it. I take a long, deep drag and blow the smoke up into the air with a satisfying exhale.

The weird thing is, I don't even smoke. Never have. It just feels... appropriate.

I take one more drag and look over at the remains of Prizrak. He's a mess. Blood is erupting out from between his legs, trickling down from chest, and pumping out from his throat. His eyes are locked wide with panic as he clings to the final moments of his life.

"And to make Satan's job a little easier..."

I flick the cigarette onto the trail of gasoline. Flames burst into life, chasing a blue line all the way to bodies. The fire catches them with a loud *thwump* and immediately latches on to Prizrak's mutilated body. His final breath was a scream, barely heard over the roar of the flames devouring his body.

I take a deep breath, allowing my rage to subside, my adrenaline to disperse, and my heart rate to slow.

Then I walk out of the warehouse and don't look back.

10

———————

I gently close Maria's bedroom door. Josh dropped me off at home about twenty minutes ago. It took us a while to get back, as we hit traffic on I-95, so she was already asleep. I grabbed a quick shower to wash away the day, but I wanted to check on her all the same.

I head downstairs and into the living room. Janine's on the sofa, watching TV. She looks over as I walk in.

"How was your meeting?" she asks.

I sit down heavily beside her and lean to one side, sprawling out. "It was fine."

"Are you sure? You don't look like it was fine."

"Ah, I'm all right. Just tired. Been a long day, and I hate having to hit the road, y'know?"

"Aww, I know, sweetie." She leans across and lies on me, resting her head on my chest and bringing her feet up. "But you're home now. Want to get an early night?"

I kiss the top of her head. "Sounds great."

She jumps to her feet, smiling. "Come on then, soldier."

As I stand, the house phone starts ringing. We both roll our eyes.

"I'll get it," I say. "I'll meet you upstairs."

She kisses me. "Don't keep me waiting."

She heads upstairs. I walk over to the phone and answer it.

"Yeah?"

"Adrian? It's me."

"Hey, Josh. I just got rid of you. What's up?"

"Yeah, well, this couldn't wait. Adrian, what you did today..."

I sigh. We had a long discussion about it in the car. The phrase 'drastic overreaction' was used more than once. Josh was shocked, to say the least. He raised a lot of concerns over my state of mind and whether we should continue doing this. But I think, in the end, he came to understand where my head was at and why I did what I did.

"I thought we talked about this on the way back?" I say.

"Yeah, we did. This isn't about that. Well, it is, but I'm not calling to shout at you."

"Then what's up?"

"Adrian, today's contract... how you did it... you're a legend!"

I frown. "I'm a what?"

"Everyone's talking about it."

"Who's everyone?"

"Y'know, other assassins."

"How do you know?"

"Because we're a part of a bigger world now—a long-standing community of killers, built on honor and tradition. And our entire world is going nuts over what you did!

Adrian, in one day, you've managed to scare a brotherhood of professional assassins shitless!"

He's laughing.

"That's... pretty crazy."

"I know! They've even given you a nickname!"

I roll my eyes. "I don't want a nickname. I'm not nine."

"Well, tough. Word's gotten around about exactly what you did. The way you finished him off... and the fire... People are calling you Adrian *Hell*. Can you believe that?"

"Right..."

"Do you know what this means?"

"We need new business cards?"

He scoffs. "It means you're top of the food chain. Your reputation has skyrocketed overnight. With a little help from yours truly, you're about to be the most sought-after assassin in the world. We can write our own ticket with this, boss—charge whatever we want. You're about to become a very rich hitman."

"That's... great."

Josh tuts. "You could sound a little happier."

"Sorry, man. I'm glad, really. And thank you for, y'know, handling that side of things for me. But it's been a long day. There's a lot of shit in my head I want to forget about, and there's a beautiful woman upstairs who wants to help with that, so..."

He laughs. "Say no more, boss. I'll be in touch."

He hangs up.

I toss the phone on the sofa and head upstairs.

Adrian Hell, eh?

I smile. Don't tell Josh, but I actually kind of like it.

THE END

TESTED

AN ADRIAN HELL ONE-SHOT

NOVEMBER 3, 2004

1

_____

Josh and I rarely disagree on anything. We occasionally clash when trying to decide the music for a road trip. The heated debates we have about sport aren't serious—I don't follow any with enough passion to care what actually happens, and Josh simply enjoys pointing out all the ways he thinks the U.K. is better than the U.S. at football. Or soccer. Whatever. My point is, we've always been on the same page when it comes to the stuff that matters.

Except today.

Today, we have a significant difference of opinion.

We're sitting in a coffee house roughly five minutes from my house. We come here all the time to discuss work. The waitresses know us by name, know our regular order, and always exchange pleasantries when we walk in. We're at our usual corner booth. I'm sitting with my back to the wall, looking out at the steady flow of customers. Josh is across from me.

"I don't understand what the problem is," he says. "It's a hundred grand."

I shake my head. "The problem is, it's not just about the money. I've always said I need to understand and accept the reasons for the job before we take it."

"I know, but—"

"And you accepted this job without giving me the details first."

"That's because you could do it with your eyes closed, Adrian. It's easy money. You should be snapping stuff like this up."

"I don't care how easy it is, Josh. Had I read the brief beforehand, I wouldn't have taken the contract."

He rubs his temples with obvious frustration. "Why?"

"Because I don't agree with it."

"Why do we even care what the reason behind a contract is? You're a..." He leans forward a little. "You're an assassin. You get paid to kill people, remember? You can't honestly tell me you feel justified in taking the moral high ground with this job."

I lean forward too, matching his body language and adjusted volume. "I know what I do, all right, and this isn't about moral high ground. It's about being able to look myself in the mirror before I kiss my daughter goodnight. Our entire adult lives, we've done questionable things for a greater good, and I've made peace with that—which is why I view this little venture of ours in much the same way."

He rolls his eyes. "You think there's a greater good to being a hitman?"

"I think there can be, yeah. If I don't think my target has done something to deserve me coming for them, I won't take the job."

"But that won't change anything. It just means someone else *will* take the job, so the target still gets dead."

I shrug. "Yeah, maybe. But at least my conscience will be clear. Bottom line, I'm not trying to save the world here, Josh. I just think I have a responsibility to choose not to actively make it any worse."

"Which is very noble of you, Adrian—really, it is. But that won't do your reputation much good in the long-term."

"Really? See, I thought the whole point of building my reputation was so that I *could* operate however the fuck I want. I've accepted this whole Adrian Hell persona you've created for me. Now I want to focus on carving out a nice, straightforward career while saving enough money to ensure my daughter won't have any worries when she's older. I figured this new reputation of mine would make that easier to do."

He holds his hand up a little. "To be fair, *you* created this persona last year when you—"

"Yeah, yeah. I know what I did, and I'm not proud of it. But the circles we move in know me now. They know what I'm capable of, and they know how good I am at what I do."

"Exactly! Which is why people come looking for you by name and offer you a hundred grand to *off* someone."

I nod. "And don't think I don't appreciate that. I do. We're making a small fortune between us, and coupled with our severance package from the CIA, we're going to be set for life."

He takes a sip of his water. "And do you not think you're doing your part for the moral high ground by not spending your share of that small fortune? I mean, for the love of God, man, live a little."

I frown, caught off-guard by the slight change in topic. "What do you mean?"

"I mean, we both know professionals who live in luxury, drive the latest cars, dress in tailored suits... embrace the life they work for."

"Yeah, we do. And those people are fucking idiots, Josh. There's no need to be so lavish and draw attention to yourself like that. Like I said, I just want my family to be financially secure. That's it. Potential customers know where and how to find us. We can exist quite comfortably—and safely—below the radar, and you know it."

He nods. "And for the most part, I agree with everything you just said. But when those customers come looking, I don't think we can turn them down based on our personal issues with their motives."

I roll my eyes as I gulp a mouthful of coffee. "It's not about personal issues, Josh. It's about the principles I live by. That I thought we *both* lived by."

"Hey, I'm all for principles. You know I am. But when we're dealing with this kind of payday, turning it down has an adverse effect on your reputation whether you like it or not, regardless of the reason."

"And you know I could ultimately care less about my reputation. Look, if someone comes to me with a photo of the man who raped their daughter or killed someone close to them, then I have no issue pulling the trigger."

"Because you agree with the kill, I know. But in the same breath, you'll happily take a job from one crime boss to kill another, no questions asked. What about your morals then?"

I shrug. "That's different."

He gestures exasperatedly with his hands. "How? How is it different? You can't pick and choose when to follow that moral compass of yours."

"It's not about picking and choosing. It's about when it

needs to be applied. If a normal, everyday person comes to us wanting a hit carried out on another normal, everyday person, I want to know why. I don't do cheating spouses or hated neighbors. That's normal, everyday shit that has no business being resolved by a bullet. But when a piece of shit criminal wants another piece of shit criminal gone, I don't personally see a downside. One less piece of shit criminal in the world isn't a bad thing. So long as no normal, everyday people get hurt, I'm all for it."

He lets out a heavy sigh. "Fine. Whatever."

Wow. I think I just won an argument! Make a note of the time and date...

I smile. "Damn right, *fine, whatever*. That's why I'm pissed about this job, Josh." I point to the folder on the table beside us. "Some Fortune 500 company's board of directors wants the aging CEO retiring early... that's normal, everyday shit. I couldn't look myself in the mirror after shooting a seventy-six-year-old just so someone's stocks will increase in value, no matter how much they pay me."

He looks away.

"He's seventy-*three*, but whatever," he mutters.

"I don't care how old he is, man. This isn't why I started doing this."

He sighs again. "Yeah, I know, all right? I know and I'm sorry. When we started this, we agreed you would pull the trigger, and I would, y'know, do everything else for you."

I shrug and nod in agreement.

"But part of my job is ensuring our longevity in this business," he continues, "and I don't just mean giving you whatever you need to keep you alive during and after a job. It means marketing, networking, brand-building... This is a business, Adrian. We're not soldiers anymore. Believe it or not, we actually have *less* freedom to do crazy shit now that we're civilians. I'm learning the nuances of our industry as we go along, so you don't have to, but I don't need a degree to realize it's bad business to turn down huge paydays for easy, low-risk work."

"There's no such thing as low-risk, Josh."

He shrugs. "No, I know, but going after a rich pensioner is less risky than taking out a drug dealer or a gang member."

"True. All right, I think we should draw a line under this. I see your point. I need to consider the business side of things more. But do you see where I'm coming from? I might be a killer, but I'm not an indiscriminate psychopath. I'm a surgeon. It's me holding the gun, so I need to be sure what I'm doing can be justified, if not by both of us, then at least by me."

Josh nods. "Fair enough. It won't happen again, boss."

We bump fists and order another drink.

When it arrives, I take a quick sip before opening the file and scanning over the documents inside. "Okay... so, what am I looking at here?"

Josh clears his throat. "A member of the board of directors reached out via his personal bodyguard, who has contacts in our world. His company has seen declining profits for the last two years, which he puts down to the CEO's stubbornness over moving away from certain markets. He said this guy's toxic to the long-term future of the company, and if he stays in charge, he's certain they'll lose everything."

I look up. "Can't they just vote him out or something?"

He shakes his head. "The CEO is also the majority shareholder. He owns fifty-one percent of the company, so there isn't a damn thing the board can do."

"And they're not prepared to simply ride it out until he

retires? I mean, he's in his seventies. How much longer does he have left?"

Josh shrugs. "They say he's showing no signs of slowing down. He's the kind of old workhorse that will quit when he dies and not before. Hence the contract. Desperate times, desperate measures."

"I think it's admirable that he's still working at his age—at least compared to the generation of slackers that will one day determine the world Maria will live in."

"Yeah, well, admiration notwithstanding, the whole *quit when he dies* thing is where you come in."

"I figured as much."

"So, your flight's..." He checks his watch. "...three hours from now. You should be in Chicago by seventeen-hundred."

I raise my eyebrow. "Chicago?"

"Yeah. Did I not mention that? Is that a problem?"

"No, it's just... I promised Janine we'd do something tonight."

He shrugs. "She'll understand if it's for work, won't she?"

I narrow my eyes a little. "You've met my wife, right?"

He chuckles. "Good point."

I take another sip of my coffee. "I'll call her from the plane. It'll be fine. Easier to get forgiveness than permission, right?"

"That's the spirit," he says, smiling. "Now, have a good read through that file. It will explain how the client wants the hit to go down. I haven't read it properly because I haven't had time, so there are no cliff notes for you. Figure out what you need to get it done, and I'll arrange for a supply drop to meet you in Chicago."

I smile. "Just like that?"

He shrugs. "Pretty much."

"Show-off."

He makes a regal gesture with his hand and bows slightly. "I thank you, I thank you." He pauses to chuckle to himself and then gets to his feet. "Listen, I gotta make like Tom and cruise, so call me if you need anything in the meantime, okay?"

I frown. "How?"

"On the phone I gave you last week."

I reach into my pocket and pull out a small, black brick with a tiny display screen and buttons on the front. "You mean this?"

"I do mean that, yes. It's a phone. You use it to call people."

I examine it for a moment before looking back up at him.

"I don't like it."

He reaches over and snatches it from me. He holds it in his own hand and stares at me. "Adrian, technology." He looks at the phone. "Technology, Adrian. The two of you will get on great!"

He tosses the phone back to me. I just about catch it.

"You're a dick, d'you know that?"

He laughs. "You might mention it every now and then, yeah. Later."

I watch him leave and then check the time. I should get going.

I close the file. I'll have to destroy it before I get to the airport, so I'll read over it properly on the cab ride there. That should give me plenty of time to figure out how I'm going to do the job and what I'll need to do it.

I stand and stretch, finish my coffee, and leave some money on the table for the waitress.

Right. Let's get this over with.

2

_____

I hate Josh. I must remember to tell him that when I get back. I'll have plenty of time to convey my feelings because my wife is pissed at me for cancelling date night to fly to Chicago for work on short notice. That means when I get back tomorrow, I'll be spending the evening alone and on the sofa.

I hate Josh.

I've been in the air maybe twenty minutes. The cab ride to the airport took longer than expected due to traffic, but that turned out to be a good thing. This job he accepted for me is far from straightforward and required extra time to process and plan.

I also need to shout at him for not reading the file himself before accepting the job.

So, here's the thing: the board of directors who hired me want their CEO disposed of in a way that looks accidental. Not necessarily natural—i.e. a heart attack—but in a way

73

that looks like a plausible accident. I did consider taking the natural route. I mean, the guy's seventy-odd, so health issues aren't much of a stretch, when you think about it. But I opted to create a tragic accident that would ultimately end his life.

Then I did something Josh didn't.

I kept reading the fucking file.

See, they want it done at the guy's home. Why is that a problem? Because he owns the entire top floor of an exclusive apartment building in downtown Chicago. He lives in a penthouse suite which, by all accounts, is something of a millionaire's paradise, filled with all the latest gadgets and toys and security systems. It's also forty stories high, has an around-the-clock security detail, and is protected by three-inch-thick bulletproof glass. The place is basically a fortress. This old bastard's so paranoid, he may as well have his own line of tin foil hats.

Maybe he's not as naïve as his board thinks he is.

But despite all that, my biggest obstacle isn't taking him out. It's how to get inside his penthouse apartment to do it. Given how paranoid he is, it's too risky to rock up pretending to work for UPS or Dominoes. I want to avoid creating a trail of dead bodies, if possible. So, logically, that leaves only one other way inside—start on the roof and make my way down.

It took me all of two minutes to read the file and arrive at that conclusion.

But therein lies the problem.

Now, for the record, I'm not scared. I don't do *scared*. I understand fear. I occasionally feel it, I damn sure respect it... but there's a difference between acknowledging fear and being afraid. Every time I take a contract, there's a level of fear. Anything could happen. Anything could go wrong.

There's always that fear of the unknown. That fear that I might not go home that night to my family. It's no different to when I ran the D.E.A.D. unit for the CIA. But that fear is what makes me good at what I do. It forces me to plan, to prepare, to strategize. Fear keeps you focused. It drives you to be better, so you can beat it every time... so that you get to go home to your family.

That's fear. It's healthy.

Being scared is different. If you're scared, it means fear has conquered *you* and not the other way around. It means your judgment is clouded, your mind is scattered... it means you have been beaten. Being scared means you've lost.

I don't do scared.

That said, I do have some... glaring concerns, shall we say, when it comes to heights. Namely, I don't fucking like them. As a human being, I subscribe to the belief that we, as a species, don't belong in the sky. If we did, we would have wings, like all the other birds.

Given I'm sitting inside an airplane right now, flying to Chicago, the irony of that last statement isn't lost on me, but if I'm honest, I'm not thrilled about this, either. I much prefer driving than flying. But I can handle planes. What I can't handle is hanging over the side of a forty-story building, staring down at the sidewalk.

And all that—the details, the location, the requirements of the job—was in the file. Anyone with half a brain would have figured out that the only way of doing this job to these specifications would be to drop in from the roof. But Josh didn't figure that out because he didn't have the information. And he didn't have the information because he didn't read the fucking file.

He simply didn't know.

But what Josh *does* know is how much I take issue with

heights. He knows that better than most, and I would happily wager the significant payday of this job that had he known what would be involved, he would've instantly rejected it.

But he didn't read the file, so he didn't.

Which is why I hate him.

3

I called Josh from the airport. It wasn't easy relaying a shopping list that would make most Republicans blush over a payphone in a crowded arrival lounge, but with a little patience and a code that probably wasn't as subtle as I thought, I managed it. That was about an hour ago. He said he shouldn't need much longer than that to arrange everything, which means I should expect a delivery of some kind any time now.

I saved his inevitable reprimanding for later. I need my head in the game. Not only am I facing personal challenges here, but I'm tasked with a difficult job in unwelcoming conditions. A thin layer of snow had fallen before I got here, and as I took a cab to my hotel, a heavier fall set in. By the time I got to my room, the temperature was approaching twenty.

I'm looking out the window, running through the job over and again in my mind. As I watch the wind pick up and turn a harmless snow shower into a frightening blizzard, I consider postponing the hit. But I dismiss that thought as quickly as it comes because I know it has to go down today. The target is scheduled to leave for his traditional weekend getaway to the Bahamas in the morning, returning Monday for the annual stockholders meeting. If he's still running the show when that meeting starts, the company will be set on the same course it always is for another twelve months, much to the displeasure of the board of directors.

So, it has to be done today.

Which means as soon as Josh's delivery gets here, I have to go outside in *that*, stand on the roof of a skyscraper, then slowly climb over the edge.

I let out a heavy sigh.

Shit.

There's a knock on my door. I spin around, distracted from my musings. I check my watch. Right on time, just like he said.

Show-off.

I pace across the small, modest hotel room and open the door.

"Huh..."

Standing before me is a woman. She's short—maybe five-three. Attractive, slim, blonde hair from a bottle... a bit too much make-up, maybe?

I look her up and down.

She's wearing dangerously high heels, lace stockings, and a long, fitted, leather trenchcoat, fastened at the waist by a matching belt. A purse hangs low from a silver chain draped over one shoulder.

I raise an eyebrow.

If I didn't know any better, I would swear she was a—

"I'm not a hooker," she says.

"Okay..."

She blows a bubble with her gum. "You gonna let me in?"

I frown, slightly confused.

"Ah... sure."

I step aside, and she strides confidently past me, into the room. Her steps are effortless, despite the shoes. I pop my head outside and glance up and down the hallway before closing the door and following her in.

I clear my throat. "So..."

She spins on the spot to face me, unties the belt, and pulls her coat apart.

I try to hold up my hands to stop her.

"Whoa, what are you—oh... I see."

Beneath the coat, she's wearing a tight, black dress with... lots of accessories. She has a shoulder holster fastened across her body, with a Beretta M9 under her right arm. A belt around her waist has a cordless power drill clipped to it. Over her shoulders is a backpack, flattened and clearly empty.

She raises an impatient eyebrow and shakes her head. "What part of *I'm not a hooker* didn't you get?"

She quickly takes them all off and places them on the bed. Next, she opens her purse and takes out a suppressor for the handgun, a spare magazine, a small tube of putty, and a diamond-tipped drill bit—exactly as I ordered.

She fastens her coat back up and stares at me expectantly.

After a few moments of increasingly awkward silence, she says, "Well?"

I shrug. "Erm... thank you?"

She smirks humorlessly and holds out her hand, palm up. "My money, asshole."

"What money?"

She takes a step toward me, squaring up. "Hey, this gig wasn't easy. I'm a fucking actress, all right? Not UPS. I was told I'd get paid five hundred bucks for delivering all this shit to you, and I ain't leaving here without it."

"You... you haven't already been paid for this?"

"Would I still be here if I had?"

Wow, this chick has a serious attitude problem! How was I supposed to know she needed paying? I figured Josh handled all this.

I absently scratch the back of my head. "Listen, my associate arranged this delivery. I figured he'd taken care of this. I don't have any cash on me. Sorry."

She holds my gaze for a long, uncomfortable moment. "Well, that's just fucking great."

I feel bad about this.

"Look, I'm sorry. I really am. If you leave me your details, I'll make sure the money gets wired to you."

She scoffs. "Are you serious? I'm not leaving here until I get paid. You can't trust anyone nowadays. How do I know you won't refuse to hand over the cash once you've done whatever the hell it is you intend doing with all this? Hmm?"

"Because... well... I won't. I give you my word. I—"

"Uh-uh. Not good enough," she says, shaking her head. She taps her lips with her finger, as if she's thinking about something. Her expression softens. Her lips curl to form a mischievous smile. "Y'know what? Maybe we could arrange another form of payment..."

I frown. "What do you mean?"

She shrugs her coat off her shoulders and lets it drop to the floor. She moves close to me and starts tracing her finger over my chest. "Maybe you give me five hundred bucks' worth of a damn good time, and we call it even. How about that?"

Her smiles creeps wider across her face.

Oh, boy.

Considering she isn't a hooker, she's doing a good impression of one!

She keeps moving forward, forcing me to step back. My leg catches the edge of the bed and I stumble, falling heavily to the floor.

"Oh, shit!"

As I land, she pounces, straddling my waist and pinning me down with her hands. She leans forward. Her breasts press against my chest. Her lips are inches from my ear.

"Relax, sweetie. I won't bite."

I'm trying to keep my hands as far away from her as possible, which makes moving her difficult.

"That's... good to know. But if my wife finds out about this, she'll probably kill you."

"Hmm. I reckon she'll kill *you* first, honey."

She kisses me on the cheek before sitting straight. She looks down at me, smiling. I probably look terrified right now. What the hell am I supposed to do?

"Look, I'm sorry about your money and any confusion, all right? If I can just—"

She places a finger on my lips to silence me. Then she smiles again and playfully slaps my face a couple of times.

"Josh was right—that was *totally* worth it."

She gets to her feet and retrieves her coat.

I'm confused.

I scramble to my feet, keen to put some distance between us.

"I'm sorry—what do you mean, *Josh was right*?"

She shrugs. "When he paid me for this delivery gig, he

said I should pretend to come on to you and that your awkward reaction would be priceless."

My confusion gives way to anger.

"Oh, did he?"

She nods. "Mmm-hmm. He also said something about this being what happens when you give him a hard time over one mistake, when he does everything for you except wipe your ass... whatever that means."

I relax a little, trying to suppress a smile.

"I see."

"Anyway, have fun with all this crap," she says, gesturing to the bed. "Oh, and apparently, the gas canister you wanted will be waiting for you on the roof."

"Thanks."

She fastens her coat.

"See you later, big guy."

She walks confidently across the room and out into the hall, slamming the door shut behind her. Alone again, I glance at the gear scattered across the bed, then move back over to the window and stare out once more at the snow-covered city. I let slip a reluctant smile.

I hate Josh.

4

I can't believe I'm out here. It's freezing! I don't think I can remember a time when I've ever felt this cold before.

Getting to the roof was simple enough. There are three main lifts in the building. The first is general access and runs from the first floor up to the thirty-ninth. The second is a private one that runs straight to the fortieth without stopping—that's only accessible by my target. The third is a maintenance lift two floors below my target's penthouse suite that runs straight up and opens on the roof. There was minimal activity inside the halls of the apartment building, given the time, so I was able to head up here with my bag of tricks unseen.

I'm just glad I brought this coat. It's insulated and padded with goose feathers. Josh picked it up from a clothing store that sells skiing apparel. I probably look a little ridiculous, but I don't care. It might not be doing much, but I imagine I'd feel a lot colder without it.

83

The sky is dark. The moon is hidden behind low clouds that are working hard to drown the entire city in snow. On the one hand, it gives me a little more natural cover. But on the other hand, I can't see shit, which isn't helpful when I'm about to climb over the side of a skyscraper.

I make my way toward the edge of the building, facing west, and look out at the sprawling, white city before me. Wrigley Field is at my back. To my left, the faint line of headlights on the I-290 flicker in the darkness.

A shiver travels along my spine.

Let's get this over with.

There's a platform, roughly eight-by-three, attached by cables to a winch unit. It's used by window cleaners to move up and down the sides of the building.

I look it over.

Seems sturdy enough.

I shiver again as another strong gust of wind kicks up, whirling snow around me.

What the hell am I doing?

Just beside it, as promised, is an eight-kilo canister of natural gas, with a rubber tube connected to the nozzle on its release valve.

I squeeze the strap of the backpack slung over my shoulder for reassurance before picking up the canister and stepping onto the platform. It rocks and creaks beneath my weight. I grip the side rail until my knuckles turn white.

I wait a few moments to be sure of my balance.

...

...

...

Okay, I think we're good.

I close the metal gate that's hinged into the rail and place the canister carefully at my feet. The control panel is on my right. Underneath it is some harness gear, which I quickly and carefully step into, pull over my shoulders, and fasten across my chest. I then attach myself to the frame of the platform using rope, with a screw-lock carabiner at each end. I clip one to my harness and the other to a welded hook on the rail. Once it's all in place, I give it a hard tug.

Feels secure.

Right. Maybe I can relax a little and get on with things.

I check my watch.

I still have around forty-five minutes before my target comes home for the night, according to the intel in the file. His apartment should be empty, although there is likely to be security walking the hall outside it.

"You've got this, Adrian..." I mutter to myself.

With my heart trying to hammer its way out of my chest, I switch on the winch. Using the joystick on the panel in front of me, I slowly start to lower myself toward the penthouse windows.

5

I'm swaying back and forth like a hammock in a goddamn hurricane up here! This is insane.

I bring the suspension platform to a gradual stop, level with one of the full-length windows that run almost the entire width of the suite. I crouch for stability and begin sorting through my equipment.

First, I put on the shoulder holster and secure the M9 in it. Ensuring I have a weapon to hand is always my number one priority, regardless of circumstances. Next, I take out the drill and insert the drill bit in the end. I squeeze the trigger a couple of times to check it works. It buzzes and whirrs into life.

Excellent.

I tap the end with my finger. It's diamond-tipped, which means it should penetrate most things. My target's windows are bulletproof glass, three-inches thick. It would take far more force than a simple bullet to break them, but this drill should be able to make a hole in the corner. It'll be a half-inch across, which is more than adequate for the next part of the plan.

I put on the gloves I stashed in my coat pockets and stand, leaning against the guard rail and placing a hand on the window for support. I glance inside. No sign of movement. No lights.

Nobody's home.

I'm not concerned about the noise. The weather out here is horrendous; the wind will drown out the sound of drilling. Not that there's anyone else up here to hear it anyway. I press the drill against the glass and hold down the trigger.

It's quite loud, even in this wind.

It takes almost a full minute to break the surface of the window, but once it does, it starts to push through nicely. The strain on my wrist is noticeable. It isn't easy trying to steady myself up here while applying the necessary amount of pressure to break through the glass. Hopefully, this shouldn't take much longer. I just need to—

Whoa!

Holy shit!

The wind just picked up, and a gust sent the entire platform swinging back and forth on its cables. It bangs against the side of the building and knocks me off my feet. I drop the drill and reach for the rail, gripping it as if my life depended on it. Luckily, the lower half of the sides are covered with metal paneling fixed to the base of the platform. So, not only can I not see what's below me, but I know nothing will slide over the edge.

One of the few comforts I have right now.

I hold tight until the wind dies down again, then slowly

stand. I hunch against the cold, and I'm forced to squint as the snow is whipped around my face.

I retrieve the drill and line it back up with the hole I was making. It feels almost completely through, which is good. I just want to get this over with.

...

...

...

Thank God! After another few minutes, I finally break through the window. Aside from a handful of slivery cracks, the glass remains stubbornly intact. Not wishing to spend any more time up here than necessary, I quickly reach for the rubber hose attached to the gas canister and feed it through the hole. It's a tight fit, but I'm able to squeeze and shove it through.

I check the time.

Still on schedule.

I turn the valve on top of the canister and hold the tube steady as the gas begins flooding along it.

My plan is simple: fill the apartment with as much natural gas as I can and then use the putty to plug the hole. When my target walks in, the first thing he'll do is flick the lights on. Doing so will create a tiny spark of electricity which will react with the gas and... boom! An explosion caused by a gas leak. He'll be taken out, and there won't be enough physical evidence left to cast any doubt on the obvious theory. Plus, the bulletproof windows should contain most of the blast.

Ideally, I would've preferred not to have to stand forty stories in the air to do it, but you can't have everything, I guess.

The gauge on the canister hits red. Empty. I grab the putty, whip the tube out, and quickly squeeze as much as I can into the gap. It'll take a few minutes for it to set, but it will seal the hole fine.

...

...

...

Right. That should do it. Now, to pack up and get the hell out of here. I need to be at street-level when—

Oh, shit!

The old guy has just opened the door to his apartment, allowing the light from the hall to flood in. I check the time again.

He's home early!

The fact I'm clearly visible through the glass isn't my main concern, however. My main concern isn't even that he's talking to a woman maybe a quarter of his age, who's draped over his arm—although unplanned collateral damage is never a good thing. No, my main concern is that his hand is reaching for the light switch on the wall.

Time slows to a crawl as his fingers stretch closer to the switch. I look around, but no options present themselves. My mind's trying to formulate a contingency plan, but it can't work fast enough. Panic's setting in.

Don't flick the switch. Don't flick the switch.

He looks ahead, laughing with his companion. Through the dark glass, our eyes meet. He freezes, his hand hovering ominously over the switch.

I see his expression harden. His lips move. A moment later, three guards appear behind him. He pushes the woman away and points at me—his mouth still moving, his face now contorted with anger.

Then he flicks the lights on.

6

___

For a split-second, it's as if nothing has happened. Light expands through the penthouse, and the panic of being trapped and exposed sets in.

But as time resumes its normal speed, an alarm goes off inside my head, telling me it isn't light flooding the apartment—it's fire.

Another split-second passes, and the noise of a thunderous explosion follows the spreading flames. Instinctively, I reach for the platform's control panel, trying to—

"Shit!"

I dive to the floor as the windows shatter and feel the intense heat escaping over me. The entire platform is pushed away from the building, and it swings out on its cables almost ninety degrees, moving laterally to the window. As I move toward the sky, I begin to slide to my left. I wrap my hand around the rope attaching me to the rail, mostly to make sure it's still there, and with my other hand, I frantically search for something to grab. I watch as the back-pack and gas canister slide out of the platform as it reaches the apex of its swing. I try to close my eyes, but a sickening fascination with the fact my body is now parallel to the side-walk hundreds of feet below me keeps them locked open.

"Holy shit! Oh, shit! Oh, shit! Oh..."

The platform loses momentum and begins to swing back toward the building. The fortieth floor is engulfed in flames. Windows below have been blown out completely by the shockwave of the blast. Some of the bulletproof ones in the penthouse remain in place, albeit cracked, splintered, and presumably weakened.

"*...shit!*"

I'm forced to my right again as the world shifts back to its usual position. My brain isn't functioning like it normally would, but it's doing enough to help me realize I'm about to hit the side of the building with a considerable amount of force.

With both hands gripping the rail and the safety harness still fastened to it—I just checked for the hundredth time in two minutes—I brace for the impact. My face stings as the mixture of heat from the fire and cold from the air scratches at my cheeks.

The roar of the flames consumes the world around me as the platform collides with the damaged outer wall of the apartment building.

Ugh!

The sound is deafening. Metal creaks and strains. I'm as flat as I can be on the floor of the platform, but the sidings offer little protection from the fire.

If I don't get out of here soon, I'm going to melt.

I turn my head and glance upward. The sky above is tinged orange. Beyond that, thick, black plumes of smoke billow to the heavens. My only option is to raise the platform back to the roof. It's not ideal because the explosion could have weakened the structure to the point where the roof might collapse, but if I can get to that elevator and ride it down to the thirty-eighth floor, I might be able to slip out of here unnoticed.

I carefully push myself up, stopping to avoid the flames. I reach for the control panel.

I just need to—

CRACK!

Huh?

I look up.

"Fuck me!"

I dive away just as one of the thick, metal cables whips down and slices through the end of the platform like a hot knife through butter, destroying the control panel in the process. The floor drops away instantly. I slide toward the edge. The harness is still attached to the railing, but the railing has been damaged, so I'm unsure how secure it still is.

I scramble with my hands, clawing at the floor, the sides —anywhere to find some purchase. As I begin swinging side-to-side, like a pendulum, my left hand finds the edge of one of the metal side panels that has peeled away slightly from its hinges. Without hesitating, I move my right arm over and grab on as tightly as I can.

Don't look down... Don't look down...

My feet find the end of the platform. I feel a sickening sensation in my gut as they slide over the ragged lip and dangle in the air. I try to scramble upright, desperate to push myself up to safety, but the floor's too slippery.

The swing is losing its momentum. It's reached its peak, and I'm losing my grip. Right now, my back is facing a four-hundred-foot drop. If I let go, my weight will snap the hook of my safety harness. I won't survive.

I feel gravity at work as I swing backward. The grip is getting easier to maintain, but a horrifying thought just entered my head...

I hope the remaining cable can hold the weight of the platform!

Trying not to think about everything that could go wrong, I glance down.

Oh my God, that's a long way to the sidewalk! I can barely see it.

My vision starts to blur. I'm not sure if that's a good thing or not. I'm struggling to keep my shit together up here; I know that. I might be about to pass out. My body might be shutting down with shock, which would be bad because I'd lose my grip and die.

I close my eyes and try to stay calm. I take deep breaths. Try to clear to my mind. Forget the height. Forget the danger. Allow the noise to disappear.

I'm a professional, goddammit. Figure this shit out, already!

An image of Janine and Maria flashes into my mind. I see them cuddled together on the sofa. They both turn to me and smile as I walk in. Maria jumps off and runs toward me, crashing into my legs and throwing her arms around me. Janine blows me a kiss. Her smile widens.

The image fades. The noise comes back. My vision clears.

There's no way I'm not making it back to my girls.

No fucking way.

My jaw tenses as I grit my teeth. My brow furrows with concentration. A fresh wave of determination washes over me. The fear of not seeing my family again is like an adrenaline boost directly into my heart.

I don't do scared, but I respect the fear.

A few feet below me, a window belonging to another apartment has been blown out. It was floor-to-ceiling, same as my target's, so the gap is sizable.

I could fit through it.

I sigh. I must be insane...

I try to center my own gravity, to become a dead weight to slow the swing. With one eye on the remaining cable, I will the platform to stop moving.

...

...

...

I'm slowing down, finally!

The heat is almost unbearable. My coat feels as if its welding itself to my body.

As I'm reduced to a gentle sway, my fingers begin to cramp from holding on for so long. My arms and shoulders ache from the strain. I'm trying to keep movement to a minimum until I figure this all out, but I glance down again at the space where the window once was. It's maybe eight feet below me. I turn my head and look to the roof. The remaining cable is taut, and I hear it creaking under the strain, even over the roar of the flames.

Far below, I hear the first, distant screams of sirens.

I'm not sure how much longer I can hang here. Whatever I'm going to do, I need to do it now.

I do what I can to strengthen the grip with my left hand and then let go with my right, quickly grasping at the remains of the railing on the other side of the platform. I get a hold of it, but it's a stretch, so it isn't as tight as I would like.

The safety harness strains against its own length as it, too, stretches from the railing to my body.

I shuffle my hips clockwise and reach with my feet for the side of the building. I use my toes to push myself away and generate some momentum to start a swing outward. I keep at it, trying over and again to push the platform, hoping the torque on the cable will make it easier.

After six or seven attempts, I feel some significant movement.

And again.

More space is created between the platform and the building.

One more, using both legs to push.

Here we go...

Again.

Yes! It's working!

And another.

I snarl against the pain from the effort of doing this.

Again! Come on!

That's it.

One more...

God, I hope this works.

I guess if it doesn't, I won't have much time to dwell on it. And...

A final big push puts me forty-five degrees from the building. The second I begin to swing back, I let go with my right hand, use it to unclip myself from the safety harness, and let go with my left...

...

...

...

Ugh!

The momentum carried me forward, and I was the right

height to drop at an angle through the broken window. I landed heavily, feet-first, in someone's living room. I slide over shards of glass scattered across the floor, coming to a halt almost completely inside the apartment. I spread my arms out to the sides and lay my palms flat on the floor for security and reassurance that I'd made it.

My head is resting on the edge. I let it hang slightly over as I close my eyes and relax, still breathing heavily with adrenaline and relief.

"I am *never* doing that again!"

I smile. Then I start laughing.

I can't believe that worked. I can't believe I did it!

Oh, man, that was intense.

CRACK!

What was that?

I open my eyes. They instantly snap wide as the sight of the remaining cable whipping toward me fills my field of vision.

"Oh, fuck!"

I sit up and roll to my side, turtling up as the deafening whoosh of the cable whizzing past damn near bursts my eardrums. The air pulls at me, and I close my eyes, momentarily frozen, hoping I've not miscalculated anything and that I'm finally safe.

Everything around me fades to an eerie stillness. I open my eyes. The room's quiet, although the noise from the floor above is all-consuming. I take a deep breath and spring to my feet. I stretch and crack every joint in my body—elbows, knees, shoulders, neck, fingers, wrists... I'm sore, but I'll live, which is the most important thing.

I pat the holster that's still fastened under my left arm. The M9's still there, which is a relief. Everything else is lost, scattered over the world below, likely in thousands of pieces. No real concern of loose forensic evidence.

Now, I just need to get out of here.

I pay no attention to the apartment. I know it's empty. I feel a little bad about destroying part of it, but I won't lose any sleep over it. No one was hurt, and I still got the job done.

I open the door and step out into the hallway.

BANG!

"Shit!"

I drop to one knee and reach for my gun instinctively as a bullet narrowly misses my head and splinters the door frame inches above me.

Two guys. Dark suits. One around each corner, at the end of the hall. They must be my target's security detail. Or what's left of it, anyway. I saw three of them get blown up when he turned the light on.

I have no cover, which means I can't miss either of my next two shots.

I stay still, as patiently and as calmly as I can.

...

...

...

The first guy pokes his head around the left corner, chancing a look.

PUH-PFFFT!

Headshot.

I hear the thud as his lifeless body slumps to the floor.

His friend will start to panic now. He won't be thinking clearly. He'll let his anger and uncertainty cloud his judgment, which means he'll—

He steps out and screams at me before moving to aim his gun.

Yeah... he'll do *that*.

PUH-PFFFT!

Headshot.

He drops like a stone. The far wall is painted by the faint spray from the exit wound at the back of his head.

That was a predictable, rookie error. He was so angry, he stepped out before he was ready.

Rule number one: you should never show your enemy you're armed while in cover.

Rule number two: you should only ever step out of cover when you're ready to fire.

He didn't follow rule number two. He stepped out of cover pissed off at me because I just shot his friend. His gun was by his side. It takes a professional maybe three-quarters of a second to level his gun at his enemy and another quarter-second to guarantee the aim. So, he needed a full second to be sure he'd hit me. His problem, however, was the fact I was already aiming at him, which means I only needed the quarter-second it takes for a bullet to reach its target after leaving the barrel.

The guy lost because of basic mathematics.

I need to get out of here. The sirens are louder outside. God knows how many more security guys are running around in a blind panic. It won't be long before other residents gather their senses and flee the building.

I don't need any more attention.

The elevator is at the end of the hall, just around the left corner. As I approach it, I see the dark, crimson spatter on the opposite wall from my first victim. I step over his body and hit the call button beside the sliding door of the lift.

No sign of anyone else around me.

I watch the display begin counting as the elevator climbs to meet me.

Oh, hang on...

I spin around and quickly gather the two shell casings ejected during the brief skirmish.

Phew!

I hear the ding of the elevator arrive.

Time to leave.

7

The doors slide open. There are two more men standing there, arms loose at their side, no visible weapons.

Everything freezes as they lock eyes with me. It takes us all a long moment to realize who we all are. I know there are two dead bodies in plain sight behind me. They will easily identify them as colleagues.

I'm assuming they're on their way up to check on their boss and their friends. Probably using the general lift as a precaution, given the explosion. It's just bad luck that I happened to stop them on this floor as I was trying to leave.

Thing is, I need to use the elevator. There's no way I'm running down thirty-nine flights of stairs. It'll take too much time. The place is probably swarming with cops and fire-fighters already. I don't want to spend any more time here than I need to.

Which means these guys have to go.

I'm guessing they weren't expecting to find trouble,

which explains why their guns aren't in their hands. I can't give them a chance to react.

I quick-step inside, closing the distance between us all, forming a tight triangle. As their expressions change, acknowledging the invasion of their personal space, I throw a short right hook to the temple of the guy on my left and then swing my elbow back into the temple of the guy on my right. They both reel from the impact.

I bury my knee into the gut of the first guy. As he keels over, I drive the point of my elbow into the base of his skull, sending him crashing to the floor, out for the count.

The remaining guy has gathered his senses a little, but I spin around and throw a left jab to his nose as he's raising his arms. It won't ever stop a fight, but it makes your opponent think twice, which is all the time you need. As he winces from the first jab, I follow it up with a stiff right to his jaw and a low kick to the outside of his knee. He buckles beneath his own weight, and I slam my forearm into his face on his way down, ensuring he doesn't get up.

I quickly drag them out into the hall, positioning them close by the two corpses from earlier. I use my coat to wipe down my gun, removing any fingerprints, before tossing it over toward one of them. Then I step back inside and hit the button for the second floor. The way I figure it, people will be evacuating by now, so I'll take the stairs with the rest of them and disappear into the crowd.

I stare at the four bodies on the floor as the lift doors slide together.

So much for minimal exposure.

8

———————

I'm outside, standing behind a cordon across the street with a bunch of other people, all looking horrified.

I must admit, it's a hell of a sight. Talk about the towering inferno... the building looks like a giant matchstick. Straight and brittle, with the tip engulfed in flames.

It's complete chaos here. EMTs, cops, firefighters, news crews—you name it—they're all here in full force.

I hope no one got hurt who shouldn't have. I feel bad about the young woman draped over my target's arm. Collateral damage sucks, and I make every effort to avoid it at all costs. But sometimes, there are factors beyond your control, and that can lead to casualties.

I make my way through the crowd and head along the street, away from the scene. I take out the cell phone Josh gave me. I hate this thing. The buttons are tiny.

How the hell do I...

Oh, here it is.

I'm calling him now.

I think.

I put it to my ear and hear the ringing.

"Adrian, is that you?"

His British accent is tinged with a hint of concern.

"Yeah, it's me. I'm just letting you know—"

"You've completed the hit."

"Yeah. How did you know?"

"Because I'm watching the news, Adrian."

I glance back at the news trucks.

"Oh."

"Yeah. Literally *any* news channel will do."

"It... ah... it didn't exactly go to plan."

"No fucking shit, man!"

"Hey! Give me a break, all right? It's been a long fucking night, Josh. Not made any easier by the fact I almost plummeted to my death at least twice as I hung off the side of a building that was on fire."

Silence.

"You okay?" he asks finally.

I sigh. "Yeah, I'm fine. I mean, I am now, anyway. I just... All right, look—this whole thing is going in the history books as a bad day at the office, and I'm okay with that. But next time, can you please read the damn file before you bring the job to me? Seriously, Josh. This was the hardest thing I've ever had to do, and it's not something I'm keen to repeat."

"Fair enough. Sorry, boss."

"Whatever. I just want to get home to my family."

"I'll text you the details of your return flight."

"You'll what?"

"Text you. Y'know... send you a text message on your phone."

"You can do that with these things?"

He chuckles. "You really are the *worst*, do you know that?"

I shrug. "I don't care."

There's a moment's silence. I turn right, heading toward my hotel.

"Hey, let me ask you something," I say to him.

"Shoot."

"My target... Are we sure he was just an old guy stuck in his ways, pissing off the wrong people?"

"How do you mean?"

"Well, it's just a gut feeling, but he seemed awful angry to see me hanging outside his window."

"Wouldn't you be?"

"Well, yeah, but that's my point. He wasn't afraid, or concerned, or shocked, or any other of the normal human reactions. He was *mad*. Doesn't that strike you as odd?"

"In what way?"

"I don't know. Like I say, just a gut feeling. Like, he wasn't surprised someone would hire someone to kill him. He had more security than most celebrities. It's almost like he was expecting it. Just makes me wonder if there's more to it than frustrated stockholders."

"Adrian, it's been a long night. Ignore your spider sense. It's not your place to get involved and start asking questions. You killed the target, you earned your money... just walk away."

"But what if there's more to it, Josh? What if me taking this job has contributed to a chain of events that will lead to something worse than if the guy hadn't just been blown up?"

"What if... what if... Jesus, man—let it go. Who cares

about *what ifs* and chains of events. You need to focus on what matters. That's it."

"Which is what?"

"That you did your reputation justice by carrying out a near-impossible hit in the worst kind of circumstances. This was the biggest test of your career, man, and you nailed it."

"I wouldn't go that far..."

"Well, you completed your job, and you're heading home to your girls. That's a tick in the win column in anyone's eyes."

I smile. "Good point."

He laughs. "So... am I forgiven?"

I think for a moment.

"No."

"Oh, come on! You can't still be—"

I hang up, grinning to myself.

I reckon I can hold this one over him for at least another week.

THE END

BROKEN

AN ADRIAN HELL ONE-SHOT

MAY 16, 2007

1

_____

This guy is really starting to piss me off. I've been sitting here for over two hours, waiting for him to show, and there's still no sign.

I check my watch again, struggling to manage my frustration and impatience.

I'm sitting low and uncomfortable behind the wheel of my rental, parked opposite a small grocery store, watching the concrete basketball court next to it. The nearest streetlight is far enough away that the darkness conceals me. Four young men are gathered just beyond the chain-link fence, standing on the court, exchanging handshakes and laughing among themselves. Two of them are familiar—I've seen them a few times these last couple of days. They're both known associates of my target. The other two are new, but they're irrelevant. The one I'm looking for isn't here.

I sigh as I drum my fingers on the wheel.

I hate this part.

Occasionally, if the job warrants it, I'll take on a contract with minimal intel that requires more legwork than usual on my part. This is one of those times.

But what makes this particular contract unique is that it's a lot closer to home than I usually go for. You know that phrase about shitting where you sleep, right? Well, not once, in almost four years, have I ever accepted work in my home state.

That might seem overly paranoid, I admit. I mean, I'm constantly honing my craft, improving every day to make sure I can justify the reputation bestowed upon me by my peers. Plus, Pennsylvania is pretty big. I know the chances of anything going wrong are slim. But that's still a chance, and it's one I'm not prepared to take.

My life, my rules.

I have a routine—a two-part ritual that I go through each time I wake up and have a contract to complete that day.

The first thing I do is something I learned as a soldier, and a tradition I carried with me during my time with the CIA—I make peace with the fact I'm about to take a life.

It's not easy. I know I'd struggle to ever justify my actions to anyone. But the only person I need to justify my actions to is myself. I'm the one who lives with them afterward, y'know? The life of a professional killer is a solitary one. It's not as if I can sit down and talk about my day with my family. And we don't exactly have a monthly meeting where we all get together and exchange notes. I do this alone.

Well, mostly. Josh doesn't count.

My point is, there's nowhere to turn if it gets too much. No one to talk to if I have a bad day at the office. It's imperative to stay mentally strong. I have to be one hundred percent certain about what I'm doing. I need to be able to live with it.

Think what you want about me, but I can. It just takes me five minutes when I wake up to get there.

The second thing I do is make a promise to myself. I don't have many things in my life I'm proud of—my family notwithstanding. But my word is one of them. It's a lesson my old man used to drill into me as a kid. He would always say, *A man is nothing without his word.*

And I believed him.

Not because he was my father, or because I felt I had to... but because I understood what he was saying, and it resonated with me. So, when I make a promise, whether it's to myself or someone else, I don't break it. And each morning, I promise myself that my family will stay safe and that I'll see them when the job is done.

Then I go to work.

That's the way I've lived my life for the last four years. I'm a damn good assassin because I keep my bullets far away from my own doorstep.

But this job is different, which is why, after much deliberation and arguing with Josh, I decided to take it.

I've been hired to eliminate a low-level street dealer in Philadelphia. It's almost five hours away from my house, which most would argue isn't exactly my 'doorstep'.

The dealer's name is Darnell Harper. He's just a punk with delusions of grandeur, from what I can tell, but recently, he's been making a name for himself around town. A kid barely out of high school started hanging around with him, seduced by the money and the promise of reputation. He started using what Darnell was selling, which turned out to be badly-produced cocaine. The kid died of a suspected overdose three weeks ago, but I've seen the coroner's report.

The coke had been cut with cleaning fluid and was so toxic, it poisoned him.

The kid didn't have a mother, and his father hasn't handled his son's death all that well—which is to be expected, I guess. The police have done nothing, and Darnell laid a beating on the poor guy when he confronted him. Feeling he had no other option, the father reached out to our community of professionals and wound up hiring me. He offered forty thousand for the hit on Darnell—his entire life savings. I said I would do it for fifteen. People like Darnell Harper are the reason nice neighborhoods turn bad. He's the reason people are afraid to walk the streets at night. The soldier in me can't let that stand.

Josh understood. He knew this kind of job was the reason I became a hitman in the first place. We talked about the fact the target is so close to my own home—only three hundred miles east on I-76. He brought up my usual concerns and rules, playing devil's advocate. But ultimately, I took his usual advice about lightening up a little and over-looked my golden rule this once.

The father had little to go on, save for a vague idea of one or two known hangouts of Darnell's, which meant Josh couldn't put together a comprehensive file on the target. I spun the usual story to Janine about traveling for business and set up camp in Philly for a few days. I've spent the last forty-eight hours hitting the streets, asking around, and putting knuckle to jaw and foot to ass when I needed to. I found out what I wanted, which has led me here.

Luckily, Darnell is enough of a douche-hole that his mouth has grown with his reputation. He's been making waves, and other street-dealing bottom-feeders aren't happy about it.

He wasn't hard to track down.

Kind of.

In two days, I've discovered almost all his known hangouts. Where he deals, where he operates from, even where he sleeps. The problem is, he moves around so much, he's never at any of those places long enough to pin down.

After a brief talk with Josh, we decided I should change my approach. Instead of simply trying to find the guy and kill him, I should establish contact with him and set up a meet, posing as a prospective client. That way, I'll know exactly when and where this prick will be, which makes it much easier to kill him.

I'm waiting here to make that initial contact. That basketball court over there is one of his more popular shopping sites. But after two hours—no... two and a half hours—I'm starting to think he's a no-show.

He's got ten more minutes, then I'm out of here. I'm tired and wound tighter than Lionel Ritchie's hairstyle. I need some rest before I—

Hold up. What have we here?

Two black SUVs have pulled up outside the grocery store. Shiny rims, tinted windows, the tuneless thudding of bass from inside...

They may as well spray paint *I'm a drug dealer* on the side.

All eight doors open. Eight men appear, followed by a cloud of thick gray smoke I can smell from across the street. Darnell's one of them. The rest must be his entourage.

Finally!

I watch as they hustle through the gate cut into the fence and over to the four guys on the court. Hip-hop-style pleasantries and handshakes are exchanged by all before the laughing and joking resume.

Twelve guys. Not exactly ideal. I didn't expect Darnell to

be alone, but I wasn't prepared for this. I have to assume they're all packing too, which means twelve guns in twelve untrained hands.

I lean forward and retrieve my own weapon from the holster strapped to my lower back. I typically carry two when I'm working, but given this is a recon session, I have one, just in case.

I hold it in my hand and stare at it for a moment, feeling the reassurance of the weight. Then I open the glovebox and stash it inside, beneath some papers.

I hate going out without a weapon.

I get out of the car and cross the street, hunching into the dark, trying to look both unassuming and conspicuous at the same time.

This could go wrong very quickly. I hate the 'acting' part of what I do, but it's a necessary evil. I accept that, but I think I hate it because I don't feel like I'm good at it. It requires patience, a natural connection with people, and deception. All of which are skills I don't have an abundance of.

Especially the first one.

I much prefer to just shoot people. Less complicated that way.

I step through the gate, slowing my pace to look around. I'm still trying to appear uncomfortable and out of my depth, as if I'm preparing to buy drugs but have never done it before.

I glance at the group, hoping to catch their attention without making eye contact. It doesn't take long. One of them sees me, which prompts arm nudges and head gestures to ripple through the pack. Their laughing stops. They all turn to look at me.

I slow my pace again. There's a small part of me no

longer acting. I'm not afraid—I don't do fear—but I'm concerned it might soon become difficult to keep up the act without feeling compelled to defend myself.

I take a deep breath, steeling my nerves and controlling the flow of adrenaline.

One of them steps forward, cutting me off from the rest. He looks me up and down, smiling an expensive-looking, shiny smile.

"'Sup, man? You lost?"

I relax my stance and let my hands hang low by my side, palms open to show passiveness.

"Erm... I hope not," I reply, shaking my head. "I'm looking for Darnell Harper. I was told I could find him here?"

The young man's eyes narrow. "Uh-huh. And who told you that?"

"A friend who is a customer of his."

He glances over his shoulder at the group before walking toward me. "That right? You shopping, old man?"

Old man? I'm thirty-four! Although, this guy's probably not old enough to drink, so I guess I am old, compared to him.

"Yeah. I've got a party coming up. Lots of people who like a good time, y'know?"

"That right?" he says again. He looks me up and down once more. "This your first time, old man?"

I take a deep breath, suppressing the urge to put my fist through his throat for referring to me as an old man.

"Is it that obvious?" I ask, smiling politely.

He shakes his head. "Arms out to the sides, asshole."

I frown. "What for?"

"You ain't speaking with Darnell until I know you ain't packing and you ain't a cop."

"So, why do I need to raise my arms? I can tell you I'm not a cop, and I definitely don't have a gun. I... I voted Democrat."

He lifts the loose-fitting T-shirt he's wearing, revealing the gun tucked into the front of his waistband.

"I ain't asking, man. You wanna leave this court alive, you put your arms out to the fucking sides. Right now."

My jaw tenses. I hold his gaze for a long moment before tearing myself away from it. I glance at his gun. It's a Glock. Possibly a 17. Could be a 19. Hard to tell without seeing the barrel.

A jab to his throat would cause shock and breathing difficulties. I could easily retrieve his weapon, shooting him as I take it. Assuming it has a full clip, I could empty it at the group in under six seconds. I'd get three or four in the confusion. Perhaps another couple as they scatter. I could be back in my car before they regroup and start firing back.

But I stay calm and hold my arms out to the sides like a good boy.

He quickly frisks me before stepping aside, gesturing me toward the group. The man I know to be Darnell Harper steps through the crowd to greet me. His skin is toned—neither dark nor light—and unblemished. His hair is cut short, faded and styled. He exudes charisma.

"What can I get you, Pops?"

Seriously, the next person to insinuate I'm old will be shot.

"Do you sell... erm...c-c-cocaine?" I reply, staying in character.

He holds my gaze, then starts laughing, looking around the group to encourage them sharing the joke.

"No, man, I don't sell *c-c-cocaine*," he stutters, mocking

my apparent nerves. "I sell top-quality coke. We're talking real deal, next-level shit, you know what I'm saying?"

Yeah, I know what you're saying. And it's bullshit.

I smile politely, trying to show I'm embarrassed.

"Good. I don't know about measurements or anything, but how much would I need for thirty people who like a good time?"

He shrugs. "You probably want a full kilo, man."

"Is that a lot? It sounds a lot. Can you supply that much?"

He smiles. "Shit. You know I can, Pops. I'm Darnell-fuck-ing-Harper, you know what I'm saying?"

I resist an eye roll.

What a dick.

"That's great. And h-how much will it cost?"

He strokes his chin contemplatively and then breathes in like a mechanic who's about to screw you over the cost of your new exhaust.

"I like you, man. I do. I ain't just saying that. You make me smile, and I like that."

I shrug humbly. "Thanks."

"So, I'll do you a great deal. You won't find prices like mine or product like mine anywhere else. You feel me?"

I nod. "I... I do. I feel you."

He laughs again. "That's what I'm talking about! I usually charge per gram, but I'll give you a bulk discount on a full key." He pauses to clap his hands, as if building the suspense. "For a kilo of my top-quality shit, you'll pay twenty-five large."

I can't stop my eyes popping wide. Twenty-five thousand dollars for a kilogram of cocaine? I'm in the wrong business!

"Twenty-five grand?" I exclaim.

He nods, smiling. "You're welcome, Pops."

"Okay. I'll need some time to get the cash together."

He shrugs. "I'll need some time to get the product together. I tell you what, Pops. If you're serious about this, be back here in one hour with the cash."

I consider protesting, but I decide against it. I'm not actually going to buy the drugs, so I don't care what he says at this stage.

"No problem. Thanks."

I turn to leave, but I feel his hand on my shoulder.

"Not so fast, Pops."

I turn back to face him. "What?"

"I'm gonna need some collateral from you."

"How do you mean?"

"I mean, that's a big fucking order from someone I don't know. I don't wanna be left holding that much product if you suddenly experience a crisis of conscience. I need some insurance."

I shift on the spot, preparing for any physicality that might come next.

"What kind of insurance?"

Harper shrugs. "You got a wallet?"

"Yeah…"

"What you got inside it?"

"Just some cash."

"How much?"

I shrug. "Not sure. Maybe eighty bucks."

He clicks his fingers and gestures with his hand. "Hand it over."

I frown. "You're seriously mugging your customer?"

He smiles. "This ain't a mugging, Pops. This is business."

I hand him my wallet. He takes the contents and throws it back at me. He nods at my wrist.

"Nice watch."

I glance at it. "Yeah, it is."

"I'll take that too."

"Really?"

"Cost of doing business, Pops."

I can't wait to shoot this asshole.

I hand him my watch.

"You got one hour," he says. He shakes the watch at me. "Tick-tock, Pops."

I take that as my cue to leave. I head back over to the car, start the engine, and pull away, heading back to my hotel room.

After three days, the time is now.

2

I used the journey back to calm down. My adrenaline spiked a lot while I was on that court. Plus, I really liked that watch.

I had a small but valuable window of opportunity. I knew exactly where this tool was going to be for the next hour or so. I knew he was surrounded by his friends, so doing this up close and personal wasn't an option.

Which meant I had to break out the big guns. Literally, the *big* gun. A Barrett M95 .50 sniper rifle. 12x zoom on the scope—military grade. A flash suppressor for the barrel, to minimize exposure. There's little you can do to suppress the noise of a fifty-caliber round being shot from a long-range rifle, but with an accuracy distance of almost two thousand yards, the sound isn't always an issue. So long as you reduce the muzzle flash, you can stay mostly unseen. Especially at night.

I checked in with Josh to let him know what was happening. That's another of my rules. Recon is one thing, but when I'm heading out to pull the trigger, I always let him know, so he's aware of where I am in case things go south. Not that things ever have, but I put that down to expertise and planning.

Well, expertise, anyway.

I'm crouching low on the roof of a three-story apartment building two blocks over from the basketball court. Factoring in the height, I'm around three hundred yards away. At a mile, I would expect to see the precise, surgical, pink mist with a rifle like this. From this distance, however, I'm about to take his head clean off his shoulders.

There's a small ledge, maybe two feet high, running around the edge of the roof. It's the perfect height to rest the rifle on. I secure the stock, screw the suppressor to the barrel, and attach the scope with smooth, practiced efficiency. I place a small cushion, not much bigger than a coaster, beneath my knee and settle into a comfortable position, ready for the shot. I flick the cover up on the scope and place it close to my eye, then adjust the dial for the zoom until it brings my target into focus.

The court is lit by floodlights, negating the need for a night vision scope. There's no breeze. The night is still and pleasantly warm. At this distance, in these conditions, there won't be any wind resistance or gravity concerns. This is a straight shot, plain and simple.

Most of the group from before is still there. I count ten, which means two have disappeared somewhere. But I have eyes on Harper. Thanks to this scope, he could be standing five feet in front of me. I move the crosshair on him and begin following him, learning his movement, his pace... all while taking deep breaths, reducing my heart rate to a slow pulse. The stock is snug against my shoulder. I'm relaxed, kneeling down.

I'm ready.

Now I just need to wait for the perfect shot.

This is probably the only time when I feel I can be patient. It's probably not even patience—it's more like professional serenity. I'm at peace, secure in my comfort zone, behind the scope, finger on the trigger.

Where I was born to be.

I watch him for over five minutes. He's pacing like a caged animal, moving around his group as if it were his pride. I have a shot, but it's not clean. I could drop him anytime, but I don't want half his crew doused in his blood and gray matter.

I just need to wait. It'll come.

3

He's just taken a call on his cell phone. I see him laughing as he speaks. This might be the opportunity I need.

Come on... come on...

Yes!

He slowly starts to walk away from the group, caught up in his conversation. This is it.

I take a couple of deep breaths, clearing and calming my mind. I move my finger to the trigger, pressing lightly, feeling the biting point, ready to squeeze. I track him with the scope. The moment he stands still, he's gone. From here, it'll take around six-tenths of a second for the bullet to leave the rifle and bury itself in Harper's head.

Just stand still.

...

...

...

He stops, facing the street... facing me. His group is maybe forty feet to his left.

I take a breath. Hold it.

One.

Two.

I breathe out slowly as I gently squeeze the trigger.

The recoil on a rifle like this is a bitch. The weapon jerks back at me, punching into my shoulder. There's a momentary flash of light before my eyes. Almost immediately, I see Darnell Harper's head disappear through the scope, vanishing in a crimson explosion. His body collapses to the ground. The phone flies from his hand. His friends rush to his side, scrambling for their own guns—for what good it will do them.

I bring the rifle down and spin around, sitting with my back resting against the ledge as I slowly dismantle the rifle.

The hard part is keeping my breathing steady. I get a rush that defies explanation after pulling a trigger. It's not a positive or a negative thing. It's more primal. It's beyond adrenaline. I just want to scream until my lungs give out, just to get that release.

But I can't.

I need to breathe slow and deep and bury the urge to let that energy escape. It's as if I absorb it, use it to fuel my ability to do the next job, and the one after that. Let it feed that killer inside me.

As I pack the rifle away, I allow myself a subtle smile.

That's a job well done. I hope it brings some solace and closure for the father of the kid who died from Harper's poison.

MAY 17, 2007

4

———

I turn off the water and step out of the shower stall, reaching for the towel hanging on the wall nearby. I pat my face, quickly rub my body dry, and then wrap it around my waist. I had the water as hot as I could stand, so the room is filled with steam. I wipe a hand across the mirror and stare at the hazy reflection.

I didn't sleep much last night. It's always difficult to come down after a hit. The worst time to carry one out is at night because it leaves you pumped until the following morning, unable to rest.

That, and the bed in this place is like lying on rocks.

Still, exhaustion won, and I slept most of the day. I woke twenty minutes ago feeling refreshed after a successful job. I should be home later this evening, and I'm going to take a couple of days off to spend time with my girls.

I pad out into the room. It's not big or fancy, but I don't need it to be. Josh always tries to book a room for me in someplace swanky, but I hate all that. I just need a room to lay low and get some rest before and after the job. That's it.

My overnight bag is already packed. So is my kit bag, containing the M95 I used last night. I'll head straight home in the rental I have parked outside. Josh can pick it up, return it, and put the rifle back in lock-up.

We rent a storage unit that we use to keep my guns and his tech. We pay cash each week, so there's no paper trail. It's rented under a fake name too. Just makes it easier than trying to hide it all in my house. Can you imagine?

We keep one gun in the bedroom. Janine insisted—said it gave her peace of mind when I was away with work. But despite having lived with and used weapons of all kinds most of my life, I don't agree with them being kept in my home. That's where my daughter sleeps, and as great as Maria is, if you have a gun in the same house as a child, there's always a risk.

As I'm fastening my pants, my cell phone starts ringing. It sounds muffled. I quickly scan the room.

Where the hell is it?

...

...

...

Got it. It was underneath one of the pillows, randomly.

The screen tells me it's Josh calling.

"Morning," I say as I answer.

"Adrian? Thank God! Where have you been? I've been calling you all day!"

I check the screen. It says I have seventeen missed calls.

I raise an eyebrow as I place the phone back against my ear.

"So you have. Is everything all right? What's so urgent?"

"You need to get out of there right now!"

"Out of where? The hotel? Gladly—this place sucks."

"No, Adrian. The city. You need to get out of Philly. Now!"

I don't think I've ever heard him sound this agitated before. The urgency... the panic in his voice...

He's not kidding around.

"Josh, what's wrong?"

"I'll tell you on the road."

"I'm half-dressed. Tell me now."

He sighs.

"Our client is dead."

"Huh? When? How?"

"Confirmation of the kill was logged a few hours ago. He was taken out around two a.m., in his home. Two to the head at close range."

"He was hit? Are you saying someone put a contract out on him? Why?"

"Have you heard the name Wilson Trent before?"

I think for a moment.

"I don't know why, but it sounds vaguely familiar, yeah."

"It should. He's the biggest crime boss on the East coast. New York, New Jersey, Pennsylvania... he runs them all. There are rumors he even has operations as far out as Delaware."

"That sounds impressive, but so what? We don't deal with people on that level. What does he have to do with all this?"

"Our client refused to tell Trent who he paid to kill Harper, so Trent took out a contract on him."

"This isn't making any sense. He wouldn't know who took the job. And why does Trent care about some low-level street dealer?"

He sighs again. Heavier this time.

"Because Darnell Harper is Wilson Trent's son."

My eyes snap wide.

"What?"

"No one knew except them. Word going around is that Harper wanted to make a name for himself on his own merit, not on Daddy's coattails, so he uses his mother's maiden name. He's kept it secret for years. From everyone."

I sit on the edge of the bed and rest my head in my hand.

"So, to clarify, I just killed the son of a powerful crime boss?"

"It would appear so. You need to lay low for a few days. Let me see if there's a way of smoothing this over."

"How can you *possibly* smooth this over, Josh?"

"I don't know, all right! But I need to think of something before…"

The line goes quiet.

"Before what?"

Nothing.

"Josh, are you still there? Before what?"

"Adrian, Wilson Trent just took out a contract on you!"

I leap to my feet.

"How much?" I ask urgently.

"That's your first thought? Does it matter?"

"Yes. Absolutely. Our code is that we never go after each other, right? That's the honor professional assassins live by. But honor can be bought. For the right price, you can get anyone to do anything."

"Fine. Let me see…" He pauses. "Fuck me!"

I roll my eyes. "What is it?"

"He's offering a million dollars to anyone who brings him your head."

"Holy shit! How did he even find out I took the contract on Harper?"

"I don't know, but he's clearly pissed about it."

"So, what happens now?"

"For that kind of money, you're going to have a lot of people coming for you. You need to get out of the city as quickly as possible."

I feel the unfamiliar and unwelcome sensation of panic begin to flood through me. My mind starts racing in all directions. I close my eyes a moment, listening to all the questions screaming inside my head, trying to single out the loudest one.

"What about my family? Are they in danger?"

He doesn't reply.

"Josh? What about Janine and Maria?"

"I don't know, but... if he has the resources to find out his estranged son was taken out, kill the man who hired an assassin to do it, and put a price on the head of the assassin who did it in less than twenty-four hours..."

He doesn't need to say anything else. He makes a good point. Trent's not going to stop until I'm dead. He apparently has the resources. I would be foolish not to think he might go after my family—if not for revenge, then to draw me out.

I have to get to them first.

"I'll call you from the road."

I hang up, quickly finish getting dressed and gather my things, then head out of the room.

Five minutes later, I'm behind the wheel of my rental, driving as fast as I dare.

5

I'm blasting back along I-76, flirting with the speed limit as I weave my way through the increasingly heavy traffic. This is the wrong time of day to be in a hurry.

I've tried calling Janine a couple of times, but she's not picking up. I can't remember her shift pattern for this week, but I know she has her phone on silent when she's at work, so it makes sense she won't answer. I'm just doing my best not to lose my shit. Not to jump to any conclusions. To stay calm and think this through.

But it's not easy.

As soon as I'm through the worst of this traffic, I'll call Josh and see if he has any bright ideas.

Fuck!

I repeatedly slam my hand against the wheel.

Fuck!

Fuck!

This is all my fault.

Goddammit!

If I hadn't ignored the rules... if I had turned down the job, none of this would be happening.

How the hell did Darnell Harper manage to keep his relationship to Wilson Trent quiet for so many years?

More importantly, how did Wilson Trent find out that his son was dead *and* who took the contract out so fast? And now he knows it was me that pulled the trigger. But seriously, who puts a million-dollar price tag on someone's head? I know I technically killed his son, but still...

I thread the rental through a narrow gap, moving farther inside the four-lane interstate and cutting off another car in the process, barely missing his hood with my trunk. A horn sounds behind me. I glance in the rearview. The driver of a gray sedan behind is giving me the finger.

Fair enough. It *was* a bit of a dick move. But I think if he knew the circumstances surrounding my erratic driving, he would be more forgiving.

I'm reduced to little more than a crawl, pinned in between the barrier separating the opposite flows of traffic and a bright red SUV with hip hop music blaring out through the open window.

I try to take some deep breaths, but nothing relaxes me.

I take out my phone. I hate this damn thing. It's some new fancy one that doesn't have buttons. It's all about touchscreen now, apparently. I'd just got used to the goddamn buttons. Josh had a geekgasm because he was able to get us both one of these new ones a few weeks before it hit the stores. I'm not sure he realized how much the gesture was wasted on me.

I start dialing and put it on loudspeaker. The shrill tone echoes around the car.

"I was just about to call you," says Josh as he answers. "Where are you?"

"Stuck on the '76, just past New Stanton. What's the latest?"

"You were right."

"First time for everything, I guess. What about?"

"A million dollars buys a *lot* of dishonor. Guys are lining up to take you out."

"Wonderful. What options do I have?"

"Right now, not many. I've reached out to my contacts, as well as respected leaders in our field, and tried to explain the situation, see if we can't establish a little decorum."

"Do you think that will work?"

"Honestly, brother, I don't know. I try to prepare for every eventuality because I know how OCD and paranoid you are about all this, but no one, not even me, could have seen this coming."

"I know. I just—"

"Ah-ah-ah. Don't do it."

I frown. "Do what?"

"Start blaming yourself."

"But I—"

"It won't do you or anyone else any good, Adrian. We just need to react, get ahead of this, and figure out how to minimize the damage."

I look around as I ease slowly forward. The gray sky is deceptive, suggesting rain despite the temperature holding steady in the mid-seventies. I look at the clock on the dash. I'm still a good three hours away from home.

"Give it to me straight, Josh. Is my family in any danger?"

"From an assassin? Not a chance. No professional will intentionally go after anyone other than their target, even if they're breaking the code by targeting one of their own."

"And what about from Wilson Trent?"

"I don't know, man. I'm sorry."

"Is he someone I can take out?"

He scoffs a little. "Are you being serious?"

"Professional question."

"No, Adrian. He's not. He has a fucking army. He's worth hundreds of millions of dollars. He has politicians and police on his payroll. He controls nearly every illegal business in a thousand-mile radius of Pittsburgh."

"You could have stopped at 'no'. I get the point."

"Sorry."

"I need to make sure my family stays safe. How quickly can you get to them?"

"I'm in Buffalo right now, so no faster than you can."

"Shit. All right. Can you just... I don't know... come up with something?"

"I'll keep trying to get the community back on our side, see if we can somehow void Trent's contract."

"Thanks. We need to stay ahead of this."

"I know."

"Josh?"

"Yeah?"

I hate to say this. I hate to even *think* it, but I need to.

"I need a plan in place to deal with *every* outcome. Every possible way this could end. Do you understand what I'm saying to you?"

He pauses. "Yeah, I do. But you can't think like that, man."

"I have to. I'm three hours away from my house. That's a lot of road to cover. With everyone coming after me, I need to accept the fact I might not make it off this interstate, let alone back home. I need you to make sure there's a plan in place, okay?"

"I've got your back, boss. You know I do. But stay positive, yeah?"

BANG!

Oh, shit!

I duck low behind the wheel as a bullet splinters the passenger door window.

"What the hell was that?" screams Josh on speaker.

I look across and see the driver of the red SUV aiming a gun at me.

Shit.

"I'm *positive* that was the driver of the car next to me trying to earn Trent's million. Call you back."

I toss the phone on the backseat and retrieve my M9 from the glovebox. The suppressor is already attached, and the magazine is full.

My lane has begun moving a little faster, so I pull away from the SUV. It's now two cars back on my right. That buys me a little time, but it won't be long before it draws level again, and as things stand, there's nowhere for me to go.

This is turning into a very bad day.

6

———

I see a gap ahead that will allow me to pull into the same lane as the SUV, with a car between us. I just need this prick in front of me to speed up so I can—

BANG!

Jesus!

I duck instinctively and then glance over my shoulder. The driver of the red SUV is leaning out of his window, aiming his gun at me. Both windows on the passenger side are now destroyed.

"Hey! This is a rental, asshole!" I shout.

There goes my deposit.

Keeping my hand steady on the wheel, maintaining the pace the car in front is allowing me, I shift in my seat and rest my arm on the back, taking aim at the opportunistic assassin.

I fire twice through the broken rear passenger window.

The first round takes some paint off his hood.

The second removes his wing mirror.

He swerves slightly, almost hitting the car to his right.

That'll give him something to think about.

I turn back around, re-focus on the road ahead, and thread myself through the gap, moving into the second lane. I check the rearview. The SUV has regained control, but he's three cars back and pinned in his lane by traffic.

I just bought myself maybe three minutes to find a way out of this without any innocent people getting hurt.

I see a sign for a turn-off coming up in just under a mile.

If I leave the interstate, I'm prolonging my journey home and making myself an easier target in the process. But if I stay here, I'm increasing the risk to everyone around me. There's no way Mr. SUV back there is the only assassin on this stretch of road looking for me, and most people aren't as conscientious when it comes to innocent lives as I am.

I reach behind me for my phone and quickly call Josh.

"Still alive?" he asks as he answers.

I find myself smiling at his apparent nonchalance.

"For now, yeah. Listen, can you view, like, a traffic report or something for the '76?"

"Of course. What are you thinking?"

"I've managed to put a little space between me and the asshole shooting at me for now. There's an exit coming up. I'm trying to decide if I should take it, or if I should encourage him to."

He chuckles. "I'm with you. Give me two secs."

I move across to the third lane, giving myself options regardless of what Josh says to me.

...

...

...

"Right, another half mile and the rush hour crush eases up," he says. "You should have a clear run beyond that."

"Perfect. Looks like my new friend's taking the last exit to nowhere. Thanks, brother."

"Stay safe, man."

I hang up, toss the phone onto the seat beside me, and check my mirrors again. I see flashes of red as the SUV impatiently jostles to each side, desperately seeking a way forward.

There's a long right dog-leg ahead. The exit branches off as the road straightens back up. Maybe a quarter-mile.

I need this douchebag alongside me on the right before then.

I gently slow down as much as I can. Another horn blares behind me. A quick look and I see it's the same gray sedan I cut off before.

That guy's going to hate me.

I fake a move left.

Another horn.

The traffic around me reacts. A space opens up behind me on the right.

Come on, asshole... I'm gift-wrapping you another shot at me... take it already...

The SUV pulls out and accelerates, maneuvering into the space. Now he's one car behind to my right.

Almost there.

I enter the dog-leg.

I throw a glance at the car beside me. It's an old lady, sitting upright with her nose damn-near pressed against the windshield. If she's younger than ninety, I'm the king of Spain.

Oh... I'm going to hell for this.

Well, I'm probably going there anyway, but if it's a photo finish, what I'm about to do will tip the scales.

I lean across and shout, "Hey, lady! Get off the goddamn road!"

She slowly turns to look at me. It's like she's trying to be angry or offended, but she can't be because she's terrified of either me or the fact she's driving over forty.

I try to hide my guilt.

This is for your own good, Granny. Trust me.

I point to her. "Yeah, you... Miss Daisy. Where did you learn to drive? World War One?"

Now she looks shocked. Still looks scared, but the shock is taking over.

Come on, move away... move away...

She slows and pulls in behind me, allowing the red SUV to take her place.

I breathe a quick sigh of relief. The shame momentarily consumes me. But it needed to be done. No way did I want a sweet old lady catching a bullet intended for me. Better she be pissed at me than dead because of me.

Let's hope they see it that way come judgment day.

The road's straightening out. I see the exit. The driver of the SUV is lining up another shot. No window to duck behind this time. Traffic is spreading out ahead. The road is clearing, just like Josh said it would.

I step on the gas, easing forward. The SUV keeps pace.

I reach for my gun again, holding it low, out of sight until the second I need it.

I glance at the driver again. His finger's tightening on his trigger.

The barrier of the exit is maybe ten feet to his right.

Be patient, Adrian. Be patient...

Wait for it...

...

...

...

I snap my gun level with him and fire three rounds in quick succession.

The first makes him reconsider his shot; the loud, dull thunk as it buries itself in his door is audible, even at this speed.

The second serves as a warning shot, firing into the vehicle but with no intention of hitting him. I want him to react—which he does.

He swerves away from me.

The third is aimed lower and catches his front tire. It bursts, sounding like another gunshot. Because he's already moving to the right, the blown tire hurls him away from me. The front of the SUV misses the barrier, directing him along the off-ramp.

The rear of the SUV doesn't.

It connects at speed, crushing the rear wheel arch. The impact sends it spinning away from him, initiating a fish-tail that he has no hope of controlling. I shoot past the exit, watching in the mirror as my would-be executioner 360s across the exit lane and careers out of sight over the edge.

I drop the gun next to the phone and stare ahead, gripping the wheel with both hands, willing the adrenaline to subside.

Stay calm. Stay logical.

That's one problem dealt with. Now it's on to the next one.

Getting home.

7

I'm five minutes away. I've hit every fucking red light there is after leaving the interstate. I tried calling Josh a half-hour ago, but there was no answer. I'm hoping that's because he's in the middle of fixing this shit-storm.

Same goes for Janine. I'm sure she finished her shift at eight. Thinking about it, Maria goes to a friend's house after school if we're both working. We know the parents quite well. She's probably gone to pick her up on her way home.

I stop at another light.

When I get home, I need to stay as calm as I can. I don't want Janine to know there's something wrong. I'm going to suggest getting away somewhere for a few days. I'm sure she'll appreciate the gesture. We don't holiday as much as we should. I think she'll buy it.

A car pulls up beside me on the left. I glance across as I idly look around, waiting for the lights to change. It's a convertible. The top's down. Two guys in sunglasses are looking back at me. I hold their gaze for a moment. Neither look away. I see the passenger's hand move across his lap. I see the tip of the barrel.

I roll my eyes.

Are you kidding me?

I buzz my window down and lean out, smiling politely. My right hand stretches discreetly for my own weapon.

"Hey, fellas."

They don't reply. They just keep staring.

"Listen, I'm having a bad day like you wouldn't believe. There's been a misunderstanding of epic fucking proportions, and while I appreciate a million bucks is a lot of money, I really need to ask you for some professional courtesy while I straighten things out. What do you say?"

The passenger rests his arm on the door, revealing his handgun to me. He remains quiet.

I sigh heavily.

"Come on, fellas. What about honor? What about our code?"

The passenger shrugs. "Like you say, a million bucks is a lot of money."

I roll my eyes. "Yeah. Right. So, how is it going to work? Are you two splitting it fifty-fifty?"

The driver nods slowly. "Half a million bucks is still a lot of money. And it makes things easier for all concerned, y'know?"

I smile humorlessly. "Yeah, I know. Okay, let's try this another way. You know who I am, right?"

I don't wait for them to answer.

"Obviously, you do. That's why there's two of you. You know who I am, which means you know what I'm capable of."

Feels weird playing the *do you know who I am?* card. I'm

not that self-centered, but I don't have time to waste taking on two more professionals, so let's see if this works.

The light turns green, but neither of us move. Traffic is backing up behind us, but I ignore it. I simply bring my own gun into view, resting the barrel on the edge of my door.

"You know what they call me, right? You know why?"

No reply.

"It's okay. Both questions were rhetorical. Let me tell you how bad of a day I'm actually having. I took a contract, which I carried out last night. Nice, clean hit. I almost didn't take the job, but something made me. Maybe fate. Who knows? Anyway, it transpires that my target wasn't who anyone thought he was. He had a powerful old man no one knew about, who's understandably pissed at the person who killed their son. Namely me. Hence the contract. My guy is trying to straighten things out with our community, appealing to people's sense of honor, which seems to have momentarily been misplaced in favor of the promise of an insane payday. Now, all cards on the table, I'm genuinely concerned for my family's safety. I know one of us won't go after them—some codes don't have a price tag, even if honor does. But I'm concerned the pissed off daddy might. I'm asking you guys to just... give me time to get my family safe. Please. Once they're out of the way, you're more than welcome to try and kill me, if you still think the payday is worth the risk. What do you say?"

They exchange a look and have a muted conversation I can't make out. Then the passenger looks back at me.

"You really think Trent will go after your family?" he asks.

I shrug. "Honestly? I don't know anything for sure right now. But let's look at the facts: I killed his son, and within twenty-four hours, he killed my client and put a million-dollar price on my head. What would you think in my position?"

They exchange another quick look.

"As far as we're concerned, you have twelve hours, out of respect for who you are. Get your shit together." He checks his watch. "Come tomorrow morning, if the contract is still live, you're fair game."

I hold his gaze for a moment and then lower my gun.

"I can't ask for more than that," I say with a courteous nod. "I appreciate it."

"Good luck."

They accelerate away at speed, taking the left turn at the junction. I carry on straight, ignoring the gestures and horns from the queue of traffic behind me.

That's the first thing to go my way today.

8

I park outside my house. I try Josh one more time, but there's still no answer. I hope to God he's managed to fix this shit.

I tuck my M9 at my back and get out of the car. Not sure how I'm going to explain the two shot-out windows, but right now, that's the least of my concerns.

I make my way up the path. No car in the driveway. She must be on her way back with Maria. She'll be home soon. Then I can relax and—

The front door's standing open a little.

What the...

The frame is splintered by the handle.

A wave of nausea washes over me. My stomach turns. My mind begins to race—conflicted between hope and despair. My emotions are going haywire, but I fight to stay calm.

I'm sure it's nothing.

I glance up and down the street. All is quiet.

I take out my gun, holding it low and steady, prepared for anything.

I push the door open gently.

I'm sure it's nothing.

I step into the hallway, listening for any movement.

...

...

...

Hearing nothing, I move into the lounge.

"Fuck me..."

My house has been completely ransacked. Furniture is upturned and broken. The TV is smashed and scattered across the floor.

The feeling in the pit of my stomach is getting worse.

Thank God no one was home when whoever did this came looking. I step back out and head along the hall to the kitchen and dining room. With each step, the dread is slowly replaced with anger. Josh said we couldn't go after Wilson Trent. I understood all the reasons why. They made sense. The professional in me knows it would most likely be suicide. But at the same time... they came into my house. Judging by the state of the place and the faint outline of footprints in the carpet, I would say four men, at least. Maybe five.

I feel the anger boiling inside me.

Coming here is a line you just don't cross. I don't care who you are. This is my home. This is a sacred place, away from my life as a killer-for-hire. It's separate from all that.

I pass the stairs. The door to the kitchen is just in front of me.

I don't know how I'm going to explain this to Janine. I

don't know how I'm going to make Maria feel safe again in her own bed. I'll think of something. I just—

What's that?

There's something moving underneath the door. A shadow.

No, wait. It's a puddle. Dark against the carpet.

Don't tell me the bastards who did this left the faucet running? That's a real dick move.

I get closer, pausing to listen against the door, just in case.

No movement. No sound of running water.

I place a hand on the door, preparing to push it open. I step in the puddle. It doesn't make the light, hollow splash I would expect. It's more muted. Dull. I look down. The liquid is thick.

I experience a moment of dizziness as I realize it's not water.

It's blood.

I close my eyes and take a deep breath. The noise inside my head fades away. The calm, professional logic is replaced by a black hole of horrifying intuition.

I'm not a religious man, but I pause for a second and pray. A silent plea to whoever or whatever might be listening to promise me I'm wrong. To promise me that what lies on the other side of this door isn't what my gut is telling me to prepare for.

I open my eyes, hold my breath, and push the door open.

...

...

...

I... I... I don't understand what I'm seeing.

How is this possible?

No.

It's a trick. My mind is confused, probably from the stress of the last twenty-four hours. I rub my eyes and temples. Take a deep breath. I look again.

No...

There are two bodies in the middle of the floor, hog-tied, with their backs to me. Their ankles and wrists are bound behind them, then connected by rope. The pool of blood surrounding them is significant. My brain registers what my peripheral vision sees—the same destruction and carnage as the rest of my house—but that's not what I'm focusing on. My gaze is transfixed on the bodies.

Two bodies.

Both female.

"No..."

I feel the M9 slip from my hand, clattering as it lands on the floor. I walk slowly, awkwardly, toward the bodies.

"Oh, God, no... please..."

I take out my phone. Absently dial Janine's number.

"Please pick up, baby... please pick up."

The sound of a phone ringing fills the kitchen. It's coming from one of the bodies.

I lose all sense of feeling and awareness. My hands become too weak to hold the phone. My legs are too weak to support me.

I drop to my knees, just a few feet away.

I raise a hand, reaching for the larger of the two bodies. I watch as my shaking fingertips get closer. It's as if I'm not controlling my arm. As if I'm a spectator. My vision blurs as moisture collects in my eyes. Each breath I take stutters over trembling lips.

I'm inches away, but something inside my head stops me from touching the shoulder. I rest back on my haunches, staring blankly. My gaze is drawn to the smaller body. The long hair matted with blood. The small hands of a child bound together with brutal disregard. The bracelet made of small, painted pasta shells fastened around the left wrist.

That's Maria's bracelet.

That's...

Maria's...

I stare up at the ceiling and scream. An explosion of primal emotion desperate for release. I place my hands on my head. Tears flow freely down my face. I scream until my lungs give out.

I take a deep breath.

I scream again.

There's a pain in my chest. A pain like nothing I've ever felt before. It feels as if my heart is being ripped from my body. As if my very soul is being torn away from me, never to be replaced.

My scream fades; the guttural eruption trails off.

I stare back at the bodies.

My girls. My family. My world.

The empty shells of everything I've ever held dear.

I rock back on my legs and push myself upright. I take a tentative step toward them and lean over. Their faces are obscured—half against the floor, half covered in thick crimson. Instincts take over. Autopilot kicks in. I begin functioning without choice.

Both have an exit wound above their right temple. Another two in the middle of their backs.

Two to the chest. One to the head. Professional hits.

On an innocent woman and child.

On my wife and daughter.

I step back and continue staring. I feel the emotion drain out of me, the way color drains from the face when you're afraid. A moment of weakness... a moment of pain is all my brain would allow me. As I stand here, looking down at two victims of a war they weren't a part of, I feel an unnatural detachment. Not just from this, but from everything. From the world. I tear my eyes away and look around at the chaos left in the wake of this attack.

It's amazing how quickly I can process things when I need to. Maybe it's shock. Maybe it's the soldier in me. I don't know. But everything looks new. Foreign. Nothing around me resembles the home I lived in. The home I built with my wife and daughter. I'm a stranger in someone else's life.

My breathing is slow and calm.

I'm seeing everything with a clear, dark impunity. Through eyes no longer burdened by the consequences of a normal life.

I wipe my eyes and nose with my hand. Sniff back the remaining emotion.

I know what has to happen.

I know what I need to do.

There's no fighting this. No option for retribution. No going back. There's no way of fixing this anymore.

It's over for me.

I need to disappear. Forever.

9

_____

I'm sitting beside Josh in a new rental car. He's behind the wheel. I placed a call ten minutes ago, posing as a concerned neighbor who heard a disturbance next door. That should be enough to get a patrol car to swing by my old house. The rest will take care of itself.

Josh hasn't said much. Not much to say.

I called him as soon as I left the house. Told him what I had found. He picked me up fifteen minutes later. We drove around for a couple of hours before finally stopping in this empty parking lot.

"Talk to me, man," he says as he kills the engine.

I think for a moment.

"You ever wanted to go somewhere you know you can't go?" I reply.

"What do you mean?"

"Like, you're standing on the edge of a cliff, and there's a chasm between you and the opposite cliff. You want to get

153

over there, but you just know that there's no physical way of ever getting there. You just have to stare at what you want, knowing you can never have it."

"Yeah. I know what you mean."

I take a deep breath. "What's the plan?"

"I don't know, brother. I think we need to think about this. Consider our next move and—"

"No." I turn to him. "What's the plan?"

He goes to speak but hesitates. Then he sighs. "Adrian, we need to be smart about this. We need to—"

"Don't fucking tell me to be smart! Don't tell me to think about anything. There's nothing to think about. I knew... I fucking *knew* this would happen. And I asked you to put a plan in place for me, remember? So, tell me what we do now, Josh."

He takes a deep breath and looks away. I hear the quiver of emotion in it.

"Fine." He pauses a moment, seemingly begrudging what he's about to say. "The plan is simple enough. We know Trent isn't going to stop. We know he knows where you live. We can't fight him, so we run. We leave Pennsylvania and never look back. We keep moving, stay under the radar, off the grid as much as possible, and we carve out another life. We have the money. At the push of a button, I can completely re-write our legal identities. Adrian Hughes dies tonight. No one will come looking for us. Not Trent. Not the police. No one. I've seen to it that we become someone else."

I raise an eyebrow. "All that... at the push of a button?"

He shrugs. "Figuratively speaking, yes. Think of it as the nuclear option in case the worst happens."

I nod slowly. "And we can keep working?"

He nods back. "We can, if and when you want to."

I look away, staring out of the window. "Do it."

"Adrian, please, I'm begging you, man. Just take a moment and—"

I look back at him. I feel the emptiness behind my eyes as if it's tangible.

"I said do it. There's nothing left for me here. If I can't bury the man who did this, I'll bury the life he destroyed. Now do it."

I turn away again. I hear him making a call.

"It's me," he says to whoever answered. "Go ahead. Yes, I'm sure. No, I don't want to reconsider." He pauses. "No, that won't be necessary. Thanks."

He starts the car. I listen to the engine idling for a moment.

"It's done," he announces. "So, where to now, boss?"

I relax back into my seat. My vision blurs as I stare at the dark sky through the window. At the city I once called home. At the final resting place of my family, whose graves I'll never get to see.

"Anywhere, man. It doesn't matter." More tears escape down my cheeks. "Nothing does... not anymore."

We ease out of the empty lot and speed away into the night, leaving thirty-four years of my life behind.

THE END

RUNAWAY

AN ADRIAN HELL ONE-SHOT

MARCH 15, 2008

1

———

Josh is staring at me. I raise an eyebrow. "What?"

He shrugs. "Oh, nothing. It's just... you've seen the time, right?"

I check my watch. "Yeah."

"And yet, you're drinking a beer..."

"You say that like you have a point."

He sighs. "No. No point, I guess."

I smile. "Jealous?"

He laughs. "Not particularly, no. Have you ever thought of trying coffee?"

I frown. "Is caffeine better than alcohol?"

"When you fire guns for a living, yeah, probably."

I nod. "Huh... now *that's* a good point."

I finish my glass of beer and push it aside. We're sitting opposite each other at a table in a bar. Well, I say *bar*, but it's one of those casual restaurants that serves alcohol as soon as they open, which happens to be breakfast time. Josh has

161

just finished a plate of bacon and eggs. I've just finished a Budweiser.

It's rare that we meet up, and this is the first time I've seen him in a couple of months. He said he would be passing through Fort Wayne, Indiana, so I jumped on the next bus I could find that came here. I arrived last night, and I met him in this bar about a half-hour ago. We didn't say much at first. It wasn't awkward. That's how we are. We're like brothers. We don't always need to talk when we're together.

"So, how are you keeping?" he asks me.

I shrug. "I'm fine."

"Uh-huh. So, how are you keeping?"

I smile. "What do you want me to say, Josh? I feel like shit. Same as always."

He nods. "Yeah, I figured. Just checking if you still feel normal. Is there anything I can do?"

"Just keep me busy. And don't give me a hard time if I want a beer for breakfast."

He laughs. "I can definitely keep you busy. But giving you a hard time is why you keep me around."

I show him a wry smile. "Yeah, one of many reasons."

He takes a sip of his juice. "Okay, I've got a job for you. It's down in Louisville, Kentucky."

"What's the payday?"

Josh picks up the thin folder that's lying next to him on the table and holds it open in his hand. He scans over the page and looks up at me. "Eighty thousand."

I raise an eyebrow. "Not bad. Who's the client?"

He nods. "It's a couple, both in their mid-forties. Both have well-paid jobs. Their daughter, Jennifer, has fallen in with a religious cult of some sort. They suspect she's being abused. The kid won't listen to reason because she's all brainwashed and shit. The cops can't help because the cult stonewalls any attempts to investigate, hiding behind all kinds of bullshit laws protecting their so-called beliefs. The parents are out of options, so they want the leader of this cult gone."

I run my hand over my head. My hair's short, and it feels coarse on my palm. "Sounds pretty heavy. How old's the girl?"

"Fifteen."

"Jesus..."

"So, you want it?"

I shrug. "Yeah, why not? You got any more details?"

"Have I got... Are you taking the piss?"

I smile. I love it when he talks British, especially when he's mad or pretending to be offended.

Josh shuffles through the file and pulls a sheet of paper out. He places it on the table, spins it around, and pushes it toward me. "Names of known associates. The address, along with the blueprints of both the properties and the grounds. Profile on the leader. Financials."

I smile. "Never doubted you, man."

He tilts his head. "And yet, you felt you had to ask anyway..."

I ignore him. I pick up the sheet and scan over it.

Jesus... how does he get this stuff?

This religious movement is called The Children of the Light. It sounds like a Rush song. It's run by a guy named Kenneth Wylde. There's a black and white photo of him clipped to the corner, taken from a distance. Definitely a surveillance shot. The guy looks like a Manson wannabe. Says here he's retired, but he used to run a Fortune 500 company before throwing in the towel on account of, and I quote, *finding God.*

Sounds like a mid-life crisis to me, but never mind.

I look up. "Do we have a timeframe?"

Josh shrugs. "The parents fear for their daughter's life, so I would say sooner rather than later."

I nod. "Okay, I'll get straight on it. What are you doing now, then?"

He shrugs. "I might kick around here for a while. They're showing the match in here tonight. It's England's last friendly before the Euros, and I wouldn't mind watching it."

I frown. "Euros? Is that soccer?"

He shakes his head. "No, it's football. You kick a ball... with your foot... hence the name. Not that sorry excuse for rugby that you Yanks call football."

"What's rugby?"

He goes to answer but stops himself. Instead, he smiles humorlessly. "You're doing that on purpose, aren't you? To annoy me."

I shrug. "Maybe a little. So, what's the Euros, anyway?"

He glares at me.

I hold my hands up. "Genuine question."

"The European Championships. It's like the World Cup, except Brazil isn't allowed to play."

"Ah, I see. Kinda like the World Series, then?"

Josh massages the bridge of his nose between his thumb and finger. "Give me strength..." he mutters, not quite to himself.

I chuckle. "What?"

He looks at me. "Americans, man... You've got no idea. Right, the World Cup is a tournament where every nation on the planet comes together to see who's the best. It's like the Olympics, but it's just football."

I nod. "I know *that*..."

"Right, well, the World Series is only played by American teams. It's more like the *American* Series. You people think you're the center of everything and need to make it sound more important than it is."

"It's played by Canada too..." I offer.

"No, Adrian, it's not. First of all, Canada is still in North America, which doesn't justify calling it *World* anything. Second, there is only one Canadian major league baseball team, and if the last few years are any indication, they're unlikely to make it to the World Series anytime soon."

I take a deep breath and roll my eyes. "Josh, I don't even care about sport."

"Then why are we arguing about it?" he asks, exasperated, gesturing with his hands.

I shrug. "Because it's funny?"

He sighs. "You're an asshole sometimes. Y'know that?"

"I do. But you're pretty when you go all British."

He shows me his middle finger, and we laugh together. Despite how long it's been since we saw each other, we talk most days over the phone, so it never feels like we're apart that much.

"How far is Louisville from here, anyway?" I ask, changing the subject.

Josh reaches down, into the bag resting at his feet, and takes out another envelope. He slides it across the table to me. "The journey's about four hours, give or take. There's a Greyhound station maybe twenty minutes' walk from here. Your ticket's inside."

I pick up the envelope and put it in my own shoulder bag, which is resting next to me. "What would I do without you, Josh?"

"Probably drink yourself into an early grave."

I stand, drop a twenty on the table for breakfast, and

grab my bag. I sling it over my shoulder, and we bump fists. "Good job I'm not without you, then, eh?"

I walk out of the bar, leaving him sitting at the table. I probably won't see him again for a few weeks, but that's fine. Neither of us are the sentimental type.

2

Louisville's a nice place. Lots of green grass and trees everywhere. Leaves are just starting to grow again, and I can hear the wind rustling them as I walk past. It's bright, but it's cold. Still got that early spring bite in the air. My jacket's fastened, and I've turned the collar up. My hands are dug deep into my pockets.

The sidewalk's clean and reasonably busy. That's the only downside to Louisville—it's a big city, which means there are far too many people here for my liking. I'm not good with people. I spend my life alone. That was the card dealt to me a few years ago, and I've learned to live with it. To accept it. So, now, I hardly speak to anyone except Josh. That's why he insists on me carrying this stupid cell phone around, so he can keep tabs on me. He's like my mother sometimes.

I prefer the solitude, anyway. It makes my life easier. I

mean, I'm a hitman. I kill people for a living. It's not an occupation that allows for many social gatherings. Can you imagine us all getting together, swapping stories of all the crimes we've committed and firing our guns in the air?

Actually, that sounds a lot like a Republican Convention.

Anyway, the ride here was pleasant enough. The Greyhound was air-conditioned and half-empty. I had plenty of legroom and a window seat. I got an hour's sleep, and I read the file Josh prepared for me on this cult and its demented leader. I use the word *demented* because my initial suspicion of it all being an out-of-control mid-life crisis was way off.

Kenneth Wylde is a fucking nutcase. He's fifty-three years old and retired. He's rich, he's divorced, and I'm pretty sure the guy's a serial rapist. There's a whole history of police reports claiming he has sexually assaulted both men and women over the years. But nothing was ever proven. If I had to guess, I would say his riches have bought him a good legal team and some airtight alibis.

He did an interview on a local news channel a couple of years ago, when his religion first started gaining traction in the community. And I'm using the word *religion* loosely. Josh pulled some details off their website, including their welcome brochure. It sounds a lot like that other cult movement that steals all the Hollywood A-listers' money. You know the one. Except this one seems to be aimed more at young, vulnerable people, as opposed to rich assholes with nothing better to do.

Anyway, in this interview, Wylde said he bought up an entire gated community in a real estate deal worth a few hundred million dollars. It's on the banks of the Ohio River and contains eleven massive houses, which he's converted into living quarters and meeting halls.

Wylde believes some long-lost god has decided to speak through him. The god is supposedly telling him to gather all the young, wayward souls and show them how they can use his teachings to find their place in the world.

Blah, blah, blah.

You know what it sounds like to me? It sounds like Kenneth Wylde is a predator who's using his money to entice young men and women to live with him in his own private Neverland. Then he brainwashes them into having sex with him.

The more I read about him, the happier I feel about killing the bastard.

My initial idea was simply to put a bullet through his head with a sniper rifle, but when I saw the layout for his little community, I realized I'd never get clear a shot. He rarely leaves, sending only his most trusted disciples out to spread his word. Plus, I need to get my client's daughter out of there. So, if I'm going to get to him and young Jennifer, I need a plan to get inside those big, wrought-iron gates guarding the entrance.

But first, I need a plan to get out. I always work backward. I start with my exit strategy, then work on the part where my target dies, and then slowly figure out how I need to do it. I find it much easier to anticipate something going wrong that way. By the time I've finished planning the hit, I've covered every eventuality, and someone dying so that I can get paid is nothing more than a well-structured inevitability.

At least, that's always my intention. I'm sure Josh would have a different version of how my plans tend to play out, but it doesn't matter, really. The job always gets done, and I always leave without a trace, which *does* matter.

This part of Louisville looks quaint, at least compared to the uneven layout of buildings that dominate the skyline a couple of miles to my right. The traffic is lighter, the people look a little older, and there doesn't seem to be as many chains or franchises around—it's mostly small business and family-owned cafés.

Josh's research is thorough and invaluable to my job, but it doesn't always give me a feel for what I'm getting into. The facts are cold information. There's no... tangibility to them. When you're out here, alone, finger on the trigger, it's an emotional experience. You have to trust your gut and learn to embrace your instincts. You need to be able to *feel* the place you're in, to understand it... how it works, how the people live, everything. No amount of paperwork will tell you that. It's why I'm walking around now. Aside from looking for somewhere to eat, it allows me to immerse myself in the city and its culture. It helps me understand it, and I'm hoping it'll eventually help me understand my target too. There's no way a cult can establish itself in a community without causing some controversy along the way. People don't like new religions. All these facts I have are great, but I'm likely to learn more from local opinions. Gossip has its place, and people tend to see more than they realize. If you filter out the bullshit, you usually find some useful information.

I take a right, putting the river at my back. The street I'm on is lined with places to eat and drink. I could happily do both right now, but it's important that I find the right one. I need something small. Not a chain. Someplace busy but not too busy right now. And it should be where the locals eat.

I spot one across the street, a little farther along, which might be a winner. Definitely not a franchise. It looks a little run-down, but it's more weathered through use than neglect. There's a small seating area out front, but the wind's too cold for anyone to brave it for the sake of a coffee. I walk on and glance through the window as I draw level. Inside doesn't look busy, with only a handful of tables looking occupied.

This will do nicely.

I wait for a gap in the light traffic, then jog across the street. Out of habit, I tug my T-shirt down beneath my jacket, making sure it covers my gun and the holster it's resting in. I push the door open and walk through.

Oh, man, that's a nice smell...

The comforting aroma of coffee and warmth hits me. I don't know why I don't drink it more than I do because I love it. Maybe even more than beer. No... wait. Scratch that. Coffee has its place, but let's not get crazy!

I let the door swing closed behind me as I look around, trying to figure out the best place to sit. I need to see the full layout, without blocking my own view of the door. But I also want to be reasonably close to the counter opposite. Whoever's waiting tables is more likely to engage in polite conversation when they don't have as far to walk back for the next order, and I need to get some people talking.

I see a small table in the far-right corner that's perfect. It's against the wall but in a small alcove. I can see everything, including the entrance, but my back's covered, which means no one can approach me unseen.

I make my way over, carefully sliding my jacket off, so as not to disturb my T-shirt underneath. I rest it over the back of one chair, place my bag on it, and then sit in the chair opposite. A waitress appears straight away and flashes me a friendly but tired smile.

"What'll it be, hon?" she asks.

I open the menu that's standing on the table in front of me and quickly scan through my options. I look up at her and smile. "Can I get a cheeseburger with fries, please?"

She nods as she makes a note on her pad. "You want a drink with that?"

"Coffee. Black."

"You want sugar?"

I shake my head as I close the menu. "No, thanks. I'm sweet enough."

"I bet you are, mister."

She chuckles and holds my gaze a second longer than she needs to, then walks away to pin my order on the board behind the counter.

I hate myself for doing that. I don't like encouraging conversation at the best of times, but I really dislike having to use charm. It gives people the impression that I'm nice and that I'm looking to engage with them in some way. I'm just playing the game. Getting information for a job is just as much a skill as pulling the trigger is. The more she thinks I'm flirting with her, the more likely she is to talk openly to me. Waitresses talk to their customers because they survive on their tips, so she's the perfect place to start.

Two minutes later, the waitress is back, holding a pot of coffee in one hand and an empty mug in the other. She places the mug in front of me. "Your food will be with you in a few minutes," she says as she pours my drink. "You need anything else, I'm Molly. Just holler, okay?"

I nod and smile. "Thanks, Molly. I'm Adrian, by the way."

She smiles back. "Nice to meet you, Adrian. I haven't seen you around before. You passing through?"

"Kinda, yeah. I'm looking for an old friend. I heard he was living in this part of town."

She relaxes her stance beside me, settling in for a small conversation. "What's his name? I've lived here in Louisville my whole life. I might know him..."

She won't because I'm lying to her, but God bless her for being so kind.

"His name's Josh. He moved here a couple of years ago. The last letter I got from him said something about him living within a religious community. I thought it was odd because he was never really into that sort of thing, but he sounded happy enough, y'know? Anyway, I was heading this way on business, so thought I'd call in on him and see how he's doing."

Molly's body stiffens a little. She shakes her head. "Well, I don't know anyone by that name. Do you... know the name of the religious group? A few churches around here are popular, but I don't know if any of them run live-in communities. St. Paul's has a get-together a couple of times a week, but that's all I know of."

I take a sip of the coffee. It's strong and fresh. It's not beer, but it'll do.

"Oh, I can't remember what he said. Something about light, maybe?"

She frowns. "The Children of the Light?"

I nod. "Yeah, that sounds like it. You heard of it?"

"Hey, Molly, table twelve's ready!" a deep, graveled voice shouts from behind the counter.

She glances over her shoulder, and then back at me. "Sorry, I gotta dash. I'll bring your burger right over, 'kay?"

I nod once. "No problem. Sorry to keep you."

She smiles. "Don't be."

She leaves, and I take another sip of the coffee. It's really not bad at all.

Well, she definitely didn't like it when I mentioned the cult. Kenneth Wylde and his multi-million-dollar sex project obviously have a reputation around here. Molly said she's been here her whole life, so I bet she knows if there's any dirt to be dished.

I sigh. Guess that means I need to keep talking to her...

3

I've just finished off the burger. It was nice. I think there were onions in the meat. Molly's just topped up my coffee too. I didn't even need to ask. I think it was a swing and a miss with her, though. She hasn't lingered at my table or been forthcoming with small talk since she took my order.

The place has emptied a little. I thought it was strange at first, but the opening times are on the front of the menu, and it says they're due to close in a half-hour. Odd that they wouldn't take advantage of the commuter rush when everyone leaves work for the day, but I guess if they've been open since six a.m. like it says, eleven hours is enough. I doubt they have enough staff to cover any more.

Besides me, there's an elderly couple sitting on the other side of the place, a woman with two young teenagers—one boy, one girl—and a couple, maybe early-thirties. If I were to guess, based on their body language, the couple is here on their first date.

The door opens, and two young men walk in. I doubt either of them could legally buy alcohol. I glance up out of curiosity and then dismiss them a split-second later. Then I register how they're dressed, which isn't exactly normal, so I look again.

They're wearing robes and sandals. Like, a full-on Jesus outfit. No belt or accessories. It wouldn't surprise me if they weren't wearing anything underneath, either. Their facial hair is nothing but poor, adolescent attempts at beards. It's not even a five-o-clock shadow. It's more like two-thirty. They both have unkempt, shoulder-length hair that looks greasy, even from way back here.

Molly appears next to me, which startles me for a moment. She leans down a little, as if she's trying to be discreet.

"See those two?" she whispers.

I nod. "Yeah…"

"They're with your friend, in The Children of the Light."

I raise my eyebrows. "I hope he's dressing better than these two."

She smiles but only for a moment. "Yeah, those guys are… pretty intense. I just hope my boss doesn't—"

An old man barges past her, cutting her off. He's short, with wispy gray hair and a stained apron. He's pointing angrily at the new arrivals.

"Hey! Turn around and leave, right now," he barks. "I've told you people time and again, you can't come in here peddling your psychobabble bullshit to my customers. You're not welcome!"

Molly sighs and hangs her head slightly. "Yeah… my boss doesn't like them."

I smile. "No kidding."

One of the two guys steps forward, squaring up to the old man. "It is our right to spread the word of our Lord and Savior. We will not bend to this... religious persecution!"

Man, this guy's definitely been drinking from the Kool-Aid. He's—

Oh, shit! Molly's boss just punched him straight in the mouth! I can't help but laugh. That was a sweet shot.

"Oh, crap," mutters Molly.

She moves toward them, but I notice the second guy is already reaching behind him.

I know what that means.

I'm on my feet and level with her as he draws his knife. I grab the old man by his arm and pull him away, then position myself between him and Molly and these two fanatics. I stand side-on, looking both ways, fixing everyone with a hard stare, which I've honed over the years to be pretty intimidating. I need to look the part if this is going to work.

"All right, why don't we all take it easy, okay?", I say.

"You two ought to be ashamed of yourselves, dressing like that and taking the Lord's name in vain."

Huh? I look over to see the old lady on her feet, pointing. Even her husband is telling her to sit down. I roll my eyes.

You should listen to him, lady.

"I do not speak ill of *my* God," says the guy with the knife. "I only question the legitimacy of yours."

This is going to get out of hand if he carries on.

I turn to face him, ignoring everyone else. "Hey, take it down a notch, buddy. I respect your beliefs, but you need to respect everyone else's. Accept the fact that some folks might not be interested and leave it at that. Now, it might be best if you left. Quit disturbing people."

He's glaring at me, but I can see the panic in his eyes.

He's still a kid. God knows why he's carrying a knife with him. Saying that, if *this* is the kind of reaction they invoke from people, it's no wonder he's armed.

I'm watching his body movements, paying attention to where he's shifting his weight and which way he's leaning. This will help me predict what he's going to do next, so, if necessary, I can stop him doing something stupid before he actually does it.

Skills from an old life, which are still relevant in this one.

I see a small twitch in the hand he's gripping the knife with. It could lead to something. It probably won't. He's too scared of me. But I'm not taking the chance when there are other people around. I have no problem hurting someone who deserves it, but I won't sit back and watch when people who don't are in danger. The way I see it, doing nothing makes you just as guilty.

I snap my body clockwise, whip my arm around, and grab his wrist. I twist it the opposite direction to the way I'm moving, which throws the guy off-balance and opens up his body, presenting a large target. It also makes him drop the knife.

I drop my weight to my left and swing back around counter-clockwise, slamming an open palm against his chest. It won't leave a mark. It probably won't even take the wind out of him. But it does push him backward against the door. He hits it hard, grunting from the impact.

"Come on, both of you," I say. "You're done here."

I reach down and drag his friend up off the floor, holding him by his neck. I open the door, prop it open with my foot, and shove him outside. Then I do the same to the other guy. They stumble out onto the sidewalk, huddling together to compose themselves.

I turn and look at Molly, who's staring at me, wide-eyed, with a half-smile of disbelief on her face. I shrug. "I wasn't about to take any chances. He was holding a knife."

I brush past her and head back to my table. I put my jacket on, pick up my bag, and then drop some money on the table for my bill, making sure I include a generous tip. I turn around to head out, but Molly's standing in front of me. Behind her, the other customers are gathered around her boss, fussing and gossiping.

"That was... pretty intense," she says.

I smile politely. "Yeah. Are they always like that?"

She nods. "I've heard people say that they carry weapons with them, but I've never actually seen it before today. They're pretty forceful when they want to be. I hope your friend isn't like that."

"Me too."

"So, Adrian... I gotta ask. When that guy was waving his knife at you, why didn't you shoot him?"

I raise an eyebrow. "What do you—"

She smiles, a little nervously. "I saw your gun when you hit the guy."

"Ah, right. Well... listen, Molly, you seem like a really nice girl, and I've left you a tip that I feel is the least you deserve. So, do you think you could keep what you saw between us?"

She looks away for a moment, then back at me. "I don't think anyone else noticed, so... yeah, I guess I can keep a secret. But I wanna know... are you in some kind of trouble?"

I stroke my stubble thoughtfully. "I'm not in any trouble, no. But if my friend is mixed up with those guys... I might be looking to start some."

She laughs and shakes her head. "Well, if this was any indication, God help them. That's all I can say."

I chuckle. "*He* won't be able to do a damn thing—whichever one it is they're praying to. Maybe I'll see you around, Molly. You take care."

I walk past her, past the customers still surrounding the owner, and head outside.

The sun's tucked away behind some light gray clouds, probably done for the day now. The wind's picking up too. I tug my collar up around my neck again and adjust my grip on my bag. Just ahead of me, those two ass-clowns are walking slowly away from me. I speed up, breaking into a small jog to catch them.

"Hey, wait up," I shout.

They look around and immediately spin to face me. "He is our Light, and we are His children," says one of them.

"He will protect us from you," says the other.

I stop in front of them. "What? No, fellas, you got me all wrong. I came over to apologize."

They exchange a glance and screw their faces up with confusion.

I'm lying. I'm not going to apologize. Except maybe to everyone else for not shooting them. But this is the opportunity I was hoping for.

"Listen, I came all the way from Fort Wayne to try to find you. I've been reading all about your... movement online, and I'm interested. Back there, I saw how those people treated you. How they looked at you. They didn't understand. But I think I do. I only did what I did because they could've turned on you. This way, you guys got out safe, and they were appeased, which means they won't follow you. I'm sorry if I hurt you, but I... I wanna join you guys."

They both take a step back. The one on my right clears his throat. He still seems a little nervous. "We are The *Children* of the Light, man. I think you're a little... old."

Cheeky little bastard! I'm thirty-six... that's not old!

I feel my right arm trying to reach for my gun, like an impulse, but I stop it. I can't shoot him. I need to stay focused and in character.

"No way." I look at each of them in turn. "I mean, you're never too old to lose your way, right? I think you're the right people to help me find my path again."

They exchange another glance, and one leans in close, whispering to the other. Then he straightens up and looks at me. "Yeah, okay. I'm Jeremy, and this is Wayne. You wanna come with us now? We're heading back to our community. Our van's just around the corner."

I smile. "That would be great. Thank you. And, listen, I'm sorry again about back there. I hope—"

The guy I hit, Jeremy, holds his hand up. "It's fine. We understand. You were helping a servant of the Light... in your own way. Our Lord will be grateful."

I do my best to subdue the instinctive roll of the eyes. These guys are fucking insane. I meant what I said to them before, about respecting other people's beliefs, and I don't mean to sound hypocritical, but... come on!

They turn and carry on walking, so I follow them. We round the corner, and they stop beside a rusty little van. It looks like the Mystery Machine from *Scooby-Doo!* There's no way that thing actually starts... Besides all the patches of metallic brown rust, the exhaust is attached to the bumper by cable ties. The small windows in the rear doors are caked with grime, and someone's traced a crude image of a cock and balls in it with their finger.

Wayne walks around the hood and climbs in behind the wheel. Jeremy moves to the sliding side door, pulls it open, and gestures inside. "Come on. There's seating. Don't worry."

I raise an eyebrow. I dread to think what state the interior's in.

I move toward it. Out of the corner of my eye, I see a flash of movement. I snap my head around and—

4

I open my eyes. Everything's a little misty. There's a constant, dull pulsing in the back of my head too. I'm guessing someone hit me from behind.

Well, whoever it was is going to be really sorry he didn't kill me.

I blink hard a few times to clear the fog, then glance down at my watch. I've been out well over an hour.

I'm sitting down, but I'm not tied up. That's the second mistake these assholes have made. Seriously, what a bunch of amateurs. Don't they know how to kidnap and torture anyone? Jeez...

This chair I'm sitting on is nice. It has a smooth, polished wooden frame and thick, soft padding. The carpet looks nice too. It's maroon and clean. A quick look around the room tells me everything I need to know. It's nicely furnished and well maintained, with soft lighting and low music playing in the background. There's a large sofa on my left, facing an open fire, which is crackling and flickering away to itself. I'm sitting at a table in roughly the center of the room.

There's no sign of my bag, and I note the absence of the comforting weight of my gun at my back.

I'm guessing I'm inside The Children of the Light's gated community. I would also guess I'm in Kenneth Wylde's own private house. I say that because he's sitting opposite me, staring at me with a wide, unblinking gaze. I recognize him from the photo Josh gave me.

There is some serious crazy behind those green eyes. I know a thing or two about monsters buried deep inside, and this guy's definitely got his own devil locked away somewhere.

Wylde smiles, slow and broad. "Welcome, my friend."

His voice is smooth and deliberate. It makes me think of a snake—soothing and persuasive.

I massage my neck and let out a reluctant sigh. "Hello."

He points at me. "As you can see, you're not restrained. I want you to know you're free to leave whenever you want."

"Uh-huh..."

"But I'm hoping we can talk first."

I shrug. "I wanted to talk anyway. I was on my way here to sign up when I got clocked from behind. I'm guessing that was one of your... disciples?"

He nods. "It was. A mere precaution. I have learned not to let my faith blind my judgment."

"Right..."

"Two of my children tell me you were physical with them."

I nod. "I was, yeah. They were in over their heads, and they were about to get lynched inside a café. I explained to them that I did what it for their own protection. I also explained that I'm in town looking for you."

"That's right." He strokes his beard dramatically. "They told me you are... lost?"

"That's me. A lost soul if ever there was one. So, can you help me?"

"You'll have to forgive my skepticism, Mr..."

"Adrian."

"...Adrian, but not many people actively seek us out."

I raise an eyebrow. "And why do you think that is?"

He smiles, as if he's about to launch into a well-rehearsed speech that he's said a thousand times before. "When the Lord started speaking to me and helped me find my true calling, I was in a bad place. I had everything most people dream of, but I wasn't happy. My life felt empty... unfulfilled. He told me I was lost, and that my true purpose was to help the younger generation now, so they can find themselves before it's too late. Lost souls don't always know they are lost, which means they don't realize they need help. You are the exception, Adrian, but I put that down to the fact that you're more aware of this world, given your age."

What a load of bullshit!

I nod along, politely. "So, are you saying I'm too old to help?"

He shakes his head. "Not at all. I'm simply pointing out that your spiritual journey may not be the same as everyone else's, and you need to ready yourself for that."

"No problem. So, listen, where's my stuff?"

Wylde pushes his chair back and stands. He starts walking slowly around the table, brushing his fingertips over the surface. "Ah, yes, your belongings. An intriguing collection, to say the least."

I know what he's getting at, obviously. My gun is understandably going to raise concerns, but I'll continue playing the part.

I frown. "What do you mean?"

"Your bag contains the absolute minimum requirements for someone who lives on the streets. There was a lot of cash, along with a nice, expensive-looking handgun. And there was... *this*."

He picks an envelope up off one of the chairs and slides it across the table to me. It's the file Josh put together on him.

Ah.

I forgot about that.

Shit.

Shit, shit, shit.

Okay, poker face. And...

I look up at him. "So, what you're telling me is, you went through my stuff?"

He nods. "Purely as a precaution. Everything is there. I have no need for weapons, and I have plenty of my own money. But I am intrigued by this."

He taps the envelope and stares at me, clearly waiting for an explanation.

Got to think fast...

I shrug. "Research. I'm a thorough guy. I know I need to make some pretty big changes in my life, and I've been looking for the right thing. You should see the file I put together on Buddhism. I just like to know what I could potentially be... dedicating myself to, y'know?"

I actually impressed myself with that one. Not bad for a spontaneous bit of bullshit.

Wylde smiles, but there's nothing friendly about it. "I understand completely. But is my financial history necessary, do you think?"

I shrug again. "It wasn't hard to find online. I just Googled you. Look, The Children of the Light sounds like it can offer me what I need, regardless of how old I am, okay? I just wanted to make sure it was all legit. You see a rich guy retire and essentially start up a religion, it's only natural to be skeptical. There's nothing sinister behind my inquiries, I swear."

He regards me silently. I can see him assessing me. I'm obviously lying through my teeth, but there's no way he knows that. As much as I hate this side of my job, that doesn't mean I'm not incredibly good at it.

I guess it says a lot about me when I list murder and deception as two of my skills.

He nods. "Okay. I think we're done here. C'mon, let me show you around."

I slowly get to my feet. "So, does this mean I'm in?"

Wylde places a hand on my shoulder. "It means we'll take things one step at a time."

He turns and heads for the door, so I follow him out into the hall. The rest of the house seems to have the same theme and décor throughout.

He walks straight outside into the cold evening. The wind is unfriendly, and the sun is low in the sky; dusk is fading into night. He's wearing the same stupid robes those ass-clowns from the café were wearing. The man's going to get frostbite.

To be fair, that's probably not the worst thing that's going to happen to him today...

His house is at the end of a cul-de-sac, where the street finishes in a wide semicircle. The other properties line both sides, all the way back to the large gates that lead out into the world. The other houses are all just as big as his and evenly spaced, but I suspect each of them has many people living inside. Only Wylde gets a place to himself, which I'm sure was his Lord's will.

Give me a break.

He slows, so I can catch up to him, then glances at me as we walk. "What do you think of the place?"

I shrug. "Yeah, it's nice."

"It cost me a hundred and sixty million dollars to buy it all. It was the last thing I did before my old life ended and this one began. Initial construction was almost complete, and the realtors were about to put the houses on the market, so I snapped them up."

"I see."

I really don't care.

Wylde points to the houses on the opposite side of the street. "I have nearly all of my disciples living with me here. Young men and women, anywhere from thirteen to twenty, all lost and looking for their way."

I'm going to test the waters here.

"And what about their parents? Are they okay with that?"

He's silent for a moment. "The people here... they're runaways, mostly. Some simply left their old lives because they believe a better one awaits them here, but most of them had no home at all. No one to look out for them. Nothing to believe in. I've given them a life here. And in return, they help me spread our Lord's word."

I wonder which category Jennifer falls under, in his opinion?

I nod. "Well, I'm sure any parent would only want what's best for their kids, right? Having them come away on a spiritual retreat won't do them any harm, and if it helps them, great."

He smiles. "My thoughts exactly. Come on, let me show

you where you'll be staying. I've had your belongings taken to your quarters already."

"Thanks."

We're heading for the third house down on the left. There's a light on downstairs. We walk up the path running alongside the well-manicured front lawn, and he knocks on the door. I can hear movement inside and a lock being unfastened. A moment later, the door opens.

I'm trying my best to stop my eyes going wide with shock, but I'm pretty sure I'm failing.

Standing before me are a boy and a girl. He's maybe sixteen. She's definitely younger. They're both wearing matching robes, which hang shapelessly over their bodies. Their faces are dirty, and their eyes are sunken and dark. They look miserable and emotionless. If I saw an adult who looked as shitty as they do, I'd put money on them being an addict.

"Good evening," says Wylde.

The two kids look at each other slowly, then turn back to us. "May His light shine through you."

Wylde bows his head slightly. "And may His light shine through you. May we come in?"

They both step back to make room, and he walks inside. I follow reluctantly. I suddenly feel uncomfortable being here.

Inside is immaculate, just as his own house was. I hear the door close behind me as I walk into the lounge area. There are six more kids—all teenagers if I were to guess— sitting lifelessly in a circle on the various chairs and sofas. Standing in front of them, holding an open book, is Jeremy. He looks up as I walk in but doesn't stop reading aloud to the rest of them.

Wylde leans close. "Some of my disciples act as preachers, teaching His word to our flock."

I gesture to the sofa, where two young boys are slouched. I had to look twice to make sure their eyes were open. "They look enthralled..."

Wylde chuckles. "They're just tired. We run many activities during the day, and we have rituals and prayer time, which can be draining at first. But it's all in the name of education."

Bullshit. These kids look broken. I'm convinced this guy is abusing these kids, and I seriously cannot wait to kill the sonofabitch.

Wylde turns to me. "If you'll excuse me, I have a few matters to attend to. I shall leave you to get acquainted with your roommates."

He extends his hand. I shake it, but it takes some effort to voluntarily touch the guy.

"I appreciate you taking the time to show me around."

He smiles. "I do the same with everyone. No special treatment, I'm afraid."

Wylde turns and walks out of the room. I hear the door open and close. I take a look around the room, looking at all the children's faces. It looks like a refugee camp. They all look so helpless and miserable. If this is finding yourself, I'd rather be lost any day of the week.

I feel a hand on my arm, and I snap my head to the left. There's a young boy standing there, looking up at me. I arch my brow. "Hello. What's your name?"

"Kyle. Are you lost?" he asks me.

"Aren't we all?"

He shakes his head. "You're too old. He won't like you."

I frown. "Who won't?"

"Our Father."

"You mean the God of Light? Why won't He like me?"

Kyle shakes his head again. "Not him. Our Father—Master Wylde."

I feel my shoulders sag forward under the weight of my sympathy. This poor kid...

I take a deep breath. I can't let myself get all emotional and shit. I'm here to do a job, and getting involved with these people will lead to mistakes.

I smile at him. "I'm sure he'll treat me the same as he treats everyone else. Listen, do you think you could show me where my room is?"

Kyle nods slowly, then walks out of the room, toward the stairs. I follow him up. We take a right at the top and head along the hall. The place isn't as nicely furnished as Wylde's psycho-pad was, but it's still new and clean.

He stops outside a door on the left and points to it. "Here's where you'll be living."

"Thanks, kid."

I open the door and step inside. There's a window facing me. The bed is against the wall to the right. There's a nightstand beside it, and my bag's on the floor next to it.

I glance over my shoulder as I move to close the door. Kyle is still standing there, staring at me. I look into his eyes. I know a silent cry for help when I see one, but I really can't get involved. I'm here for Jennifer and to kill Wylde—hopefully without anyone seeing or hearing anything.

I shoo him away with my hand. "What are you waiting for, kid? A tip? Get outta here."

I push the door shut and sit down on the edge of the bed. I quickly look through my bag.

Shit.

Wylde was lying. Almost everything's still here. Except my gun and cell phone.

5

I've been lying on the bed for a while. I got some sleep while I could, but now I just feel like I'm wasting time. I need to figure out where Jennifer is, and I need to get to Wylde quietly and take him out.

I feel bad about Kyle before too. I was out of line for being so cold with him.

I sit up and swing my legs over the side. I run a hand over my face, gently rubbing my eyes.

Don't get involved, Adrian. Don't get involved.

I get to my feet.

Damn it.

I'm going to find him and apologize. He looked as if he wanted help. Let's say he needs it. Who am I to ignore him? If I choose not to help when I'm able to, how am I any less guilty than Wylde?

I open the door quietly and step out into the hall. I can hear the murmur of conversation from downstairs. I make my way down and walk into the lounge. Some of the younger kids have gone—maybe to bed, given the time. Jeremy is sitting on a sofa, talking to a girl. She's older than most I've seen around here, but I suspect she would still be asked for ID in a bar.

They fall silent and turn to look at me as I walk in. I wave casually. "Hey."

No response.

"I'm looking for Kyle. Either of you seen him?"

Still nothing.

Jeez, I get a better reception in police stations.

"Okay. Thanks anyway, I guess."

I turn and head out of the room, in search of the kitchen.

"Why are you here?"

The question stops me. I look over my shoulder. Jeremy's on his feet, his arms folded across his chest.

I turn to face him. "I've already told you why I'm here."

"I don't believe you. You're up to something. Are you a reporter? Or a cop?"

I raise an eyebrow. "No. But why would it matter if I was?"

"Because Master Wylde deserves privacy and respect!"

His sudden change in tone surprises me. He sounds passionate, and he seems quick to defend Wylde.

I take a step toward him. "What makes you think a reporter or a cop would be here, anyway? Why would they care about a small-town religious movement?"

He goes to speak but catches the words. He takes a breath and remains silent. It's not stubbornness, I don't think. He's not defying me or proving a point. He can't keep eye contact. No... he's been trained to stay silent. It's not a choice. It's an order.

His little outburst just then was a mistake, and now he feels bad about it.

Interesting.

I look at the girl. "What about you? Do you think people would try to sneak in here for some reason?"

"She doesn't know anything."

Jeremy cut her off before she could speak. She looks away.

I narrow my eyes. "You say that as if there's something *to* know. What aren't you telling me?"

"No... I—"

I move quickly, taking giant steps toward him. Within a second or two, I'm standing in front of him, almost nose to nose. Well, figuratively speaking—he's about six inches shorter than me.

"What does Wylde do to these kids?"

Jeremy squirms backward as much as he can, but he's pinned against the wall.

I point a finger at his face. "Don't lie to me. I hurt you in the café earlier today, and that was to protect you. Imagine what I could do if I decided you were pissing me off?"

Sweat's forming rapidly on his brow. The smell is unpleasant, to say the least. His breathing is getting faster. "I... I... I don't know what you want me to say."

Well, I guess it's now or never. I don't want to spend another minute in this Godforsaken place.

"Tell me where I can find Jennifer."

Jeremy frowns. "Who?"

I grab a handful of his robe, just below his throat, and push him hard against the wall. "See, now you're pissing me off..."

"What? What? I don't know a Jennifer... Wait—do you mean Jenny?"

I roll my eyes. "That's typically short for Jennifer, yeah."

"Do you know her?"

"Where is she?"

He frowns, as if it's a stupid question. "She's with Wylde."

I let go of him and take a step back. "In his house? Does she live there with him?"

He shrugs. "Well, yeah."

I sigh. "Don't treat me like I'm an idiot."

The girl on the sofa stands and moves next to me. "She's his wife."

What?

"His wife? She's fifteen fucking years old!"

"Master Wylde said our Lord chose her for him. That she was special."

I walk away, clenching and unclenching my fists repeatedly, trying to subdue the rage inside of me. "Right, I want you both to listen to me very carefully. I want you both to go to your rooms and stay there. You don't say anything to anyone, understand?"

Jeremy looks in shock.

"What?" I ask.

"I... I don't... Who are you? Are you even lost? Really."

I take a deep breath. "More than you could ever imagine."

I turn and walk outside, carefully opening and closing the front door. Those two probably won't do as I asked, but it doesn't matter. By tomorrow, I'll be long gone.

I walk along the street toward Wylde's house. There's a light on upstairs. I glance around as I approach, but there's no sign of life. The place is a ghost town outside.

I crouch a little as I make my way around the back, making sure I'm below any windows. I work my way slowly and quietly toward the back door. I take another look around, but I'm all alone.

I carefully grip the handle. I'm hoping The Children of the Light aren't big on home security. I turn it slowly, and...

...

...

...

I'm in.

I leave the door open. Closing it would cause too much noise, and it's unlikely anyone is going to interrupt me. Plus, it's a fast way out if I need it. The few seconds I'll save not having to re-open it could make all the difference.

Like I said, I always plan my exit first.

I'm standing in the kitchen. Even with the lights off, I can still see pretty well. I take a quick look around, and—

Holy shit!

This place looks like a goddamn chemistry lab! What the hell?

I move silently over to the counter lining the right-hand wall, facing a door that leads out into the hall. There's a stand holding some glass beakers, all linked via some tubing, which leads to another glass jar at the end, filled with liquid. Bottles of pills are standing in two groups beside it. I pick one from each pile up and read the back label.

Flunitrazepam and... Diazepam.

They mean nothing to me.

Wait.

I turn the bottle in my hand and read the prescription label on the front.

You're kidding me!

Rohypnol and Valium.

I frown and look at the chemistry set again.

Hang on... is he...

The sonofabitch is making a cocktail out of these drugs. I bet he makes them all drink it too. That's why they look like extras from *Night of the Living Dead*.

I thought all the lines about drinking the Kool-Aid were just euphemisms. This guy's actually making them drink this shit, so they'll be more... I don't know, compliant? The sick bastard.

There's a full bottle of liquid on the far end of the counter. I pick it up and walk into the hall. I'm lucky the carpet is so thick and new; it's masking my footsteps. I make my way carefully up the stairs.

This will all be over in a few minutes.

Upstairs is bathed in darkness, save for a strip of light shining out from under the first door along. I stop outside it and listen. I can hear faint voices inside. I find myself squinting as I concentrate, as if that will allow me to hear better.

"It is His will, child. His light will shine through you."

That's Wylde.

No prizes for guessing who he's talking to.

Piece of shit.

I push the door open hard and step inside. I pay no attention to anything besides him. He's standing at the side of his bed. Thankfully, his robe's still on. He spins around, his eyes wide, no doubt startled by my intrusion.

I see a girl sitting on the bed out of the corner of my eye. It must be Jennifer. I don't look at her. I stay focused on Wylde. I rush toward him and grab his throat. He clutches desperately at my hand, but it's not going to make a difference. He preys on the weak, manipulates the young and impressionable. That doesn't make him strong. That makes him a coward. A depraved old man, barely passable as human.

I'm a professional, and I've spent many years teaching myself how to bury my emotions, so I can remain objective when carrying out a hit. I'm not in denial about it. I know what I do is bad. But when my job is to rid the world of an evil bastard like Kenneth Wylde, sometimes it's hard not to enjoy it just a little bit.

I squeeze tightly, being careful not to leave any bruising, and force him backward, pushing him down onto the bed.

He gasps. "Wh-what are... you... doing?"

I look him dead in the eye. "My job." With one hand, I unscrew the top off the bottle from downstairs and lean over him. "Now, open wide, you sick fuck."

I turn my palm upward slightly, so I'm cupping his mandible, and squeeze just below his cheekbones. His face contorts, forcing his mouth open. I pour the entire contents of the bottle down his gullet.

I don't know much about chemistry. I know a few people in my profession prefer the chemical approach to assassinating someone, but I'm a little more basic than that. I favor guns. Less complicated. That said, I know a little bit. For example, this concoction of his—I reckon there were two hundred and fifty mils in the bottle. Knowing what's in it, he probably put no more than a teaspoon of it in whatever drink he gave them. Enough to keep them docile and obedient. What he's just ingested is most likely a lethal dose.

Shame.

He chokes and spits as best he can, but the second the bottle is empty, I drop it on the floor and place my hand over his mouth.

"Swallow it."

I clamp down hard; making sure my finger is against his

nose, blocking his airway completely. He'll have no choice but to swallow it all. Otherwise, he'll drown.

He struggles against my grip, but it's getting him nowhere, and I can see from the panic in his eyes that he knows it. He finally swallows, and I let him go, so he can get some air. He falls to the floor, resting on all fours as he gulps in desperate breaths.

He'll be dead in a few minutes, so I need to work fast. Forensic teams can tell if a body's been moved posthumously. I lean down and slam an open hand, palm first, into the side of his face, along the jawline. Again, it's an effective strike, but it won't leave any marks.

He slams into the side of the bed and drops flat on the floor. He's not out of it, but in his current state, it'll be more than enough to subdue him. I straighten up and finally look at Jennifer.

My God...

I'm grateful she's still wearing her robe, but there are patches of blood in places I don't want to look. Her hair is unkempt and dirty, and her eyes are bloodshot and stained with tears.

Slowly, I hold out a hand to her. "Jennifer, can you hear me?"

I get nothing.

"Your parents sent me to bring you home."

Her head twitches ever so slightly, as if vaguely recognizing the word *parent*.

I step closer and grab hold of her arm. "Jennifer, listen to me. You're safe now, okay? Whatever you've been through... it's over. But I need you to come with me, right now."

She slowly turns her head and stares at me. Her gaze is unblinking, and it's a little freaky—like something out of *The Exorcist*.

I take the fact that she's moved as a sign she heard me. I pull her arm, signaling her to move. She shuffles off the bed and stands beside me. I put my hands on her shoulders and maneuver her away to the left.

"Just stand right there, okay? This won't take a moment."

I lean down and wrap my arms around Wylde's waist. I hoist him up onto the bed, roll him into the middle, and position his arms and legs so that he's lying spread-eagled. I take a quick look around the room and see a set of drawers on the opposite side of the bed. I move over and open each one in turn, quickly rummaging through them until I find...

These.

Belts. Only two of them, but it'll do.

I would've preferred to secure both wrists and both ankles, but the fact that his legs will be free shouldn't make a difference. I move back over to him and quickly fasten a belt around each wrist, tying him to the headboard.

I stand at the end to admire my handiwork.

Yeah... to anyone who finds him, it'll look like he died of a drug overdose—which is true—while engaging in some form of depraved sex act—which isn't true, but I'm figuring it isn't much of a stretch, given we've established that he's a sick fuck.

Okay, I'm done.

Oh, wait. No, I'm not.

I look around the room again. He must have them here somewhere...

...

...

...

Got them.

There's a chair resting beside a low table underneath the window. On it is my gun, still in its holster, and my cell phone. I knew he must have kept them close. I fasten the strap around my waist, adjust it for comfort, and then cover it with my jacket. I shove the cell in my pocket for now, then turn to look at Jennifer.

She hasn't moved.

I scoop her up, like a father would his young child, and tilt her so that her head rests into my shoulder. She doesn't need to see any more of this place.

As I reach the door, I hear a groan behind me. I spin around to see Wylde moving his head around in a slow, dazed circular motion. His eyes are glazed over. I think he's trying to speak, but he can't form any words. He just makes that groaning noise.

He starts coughing.

Oh, and throwing up. Lovely.

More coughing. And gasping. He's trying to clutch at his throat, but he can't.

If I were to guess, I would say he's choking on his own vomit right now. I grimace slightly. I'm not squeamish. I'm actually quite enjoying watching him suffer and die. But the noises he's making are a little uncomfortable and loud.

Oh, hang on...

...

...

...

Yeah, he's dead.

I carry Jennifer out of the room, down the stairs, and into the dining room where I woke up a few hours ago. I sit her down on the sofa facing the fire and take out my cell.

"Just wait here a sec, okay?"

I walk away, dialing a number from memory.

"Yeah?" says a voice after a few rings.

"Josh, it's me. The job's done. Looks like he OD'd. I've

got the girl too. She's in a bad way, but she'll be okay. Get me some transportation, would you? I'll leave her at a hospital on my way out of town."

"You got it," he says. "Good work, Boss."

I pause for a moment.

"Listen, give me an hour to get clear, then place an anonymous call to 911," I say. "There are a bunch of drugged-out kids in that place that need help. I can't just... I can't leave them there to fend for themselves."

"Sure thing," says Josh quietly. "Leave it to me. Get yourself and little Jennifer out of there, yeah?"

I sigh wearily. "Yeah. See ya."

I end the call and walk back over to Jennifer. I scoop her back up in my arms, head through into the kitchen, and out the back door into the cold, unforgiving night.

I glance down at her. She's already asleep.

"Come on, kid. Let's get you home."

THE END

NOWHERE

AN ADRIAN HELL ONE-SHOT

JANUARY 13, 2010

1

??:??

The cell door rolls noisily on its rusted mechanisms. A loud, metallic clang sounds out as it slams shut. The electronic lock clicks a second later. I'm sitting on my bed, resting against the cold, unforgiving wall, wrapped in every blanket I was given when I got here. The temperature is unholy. You ever heard the phrase *when hell freezes over*? Well, when it does, it'll feel a lot like this place.

Across from me, dressed in a matching charcoal-gray jumpsuit, is my cellmate, Fedorov. He's clearly more familiar with the weather than I am. He has a few buttons unfastened and his sleeves rolled up, displaying faded, illegible tattoos.

I have no clue what time it is. There aren't any clocks in here. It's part of the sentence. You get a small window, so you know if it's day or night, but that's it. There's no sense of time. Your only option is to trust that, when you've served your last day, someone will tell you. It's cruel but effective.

I've been here four days, so I still have a rough idea of the date, but I've already found myself losing track of the hours. Judging by how much light is shining through the window, I would say it's mid-afternoon, but all the snow outside makes it seem brighter than it is, so it could be later. Either way, it'll be dark soon.

I know what you're thinking. Me... prison... I must've messed up somewhere, right? Wrong. I don't make mistakes. I'm on a job. Granted, you could argue, given the circumstances, it was a mistake taking this damn contract in the first place. I'm stuck in a Siberian hellhole, surrounded by all kinds of Russian gangsters—and I'm talking about some real, mean sonsofbitches.

I'm here because a Russian mobster is paying me—frankly, *way* too much—to voluntarily put myself in this shithole so I can kill another Russian mobster. That part was easy enough. There's not much in the way of civilization in this part of the world, but there's a small town about ten miles from here with a bar that's frequented by the guards. It took me about five minutes and as many shots of vodka to piss one of them off enough to get my ass hauled over here.

I have the guy's word that he'll pull all the necessary strings needed to get me out again once the job is done. He also assured me there is at least one guard in here who knows who I am and why I'm here, which is something, I guess.

Josh was against it from the start. I'm sitting here, freezing and hungry, thinking he might have been right. But, half a million dollars for one hit isn't the kind of payday you turn away. I've had a successful couple of years, and I've made quite a name for myself among the world's criminal fraternities. I'm borderline legendary in the States nowadays, and word of my skills has started spreading to Europe and even as far east as Russia and China.

My client contacted Josh personally, which is rare but not unheard of. The guy made a compelling offer, but Josh insisted I turn it down. He said I shouldn't trust the guy. He also voiced his concern that the payday was clouding my judgment. I pointed out that I already have more money than I could ever spend, and it's never been about the finances for me anyway—which he knows all too well. Still, it's hard to deny it's an attractive offer, whatever the risks. At the rate I've been going, it's almost three months' work in one hit. Plus, if I pull this off, it could lead to a whole new range of clientele in this part of the world.

But still, Josh didn't like it, and yet again, it seems he was right. I'm just glad he's not here to see it. I haven't felt this miserable in a while. Still, I have a couple of things to distract me. One is figuring out how to kill my target in a building half-full of his friends when I have nowhere to hide. The other is how I'm going to stay alive long enough to do the first thing.

There aren't many Americans in here. In fact, I haven't seen anyone who isn't Russian. I kind of... stand out. Consequently, I'm trying to keep my head down, stay out of trouble, and remain as anonymous and invisible as possible until it's time to carry out my hit.

It's not the easiest thing I've ever tried to do.

Fedorov is pacing back and forth like a caged animal, staring angrily at either the wall or the bars, depending which way he's facing. He's a big guy. Taller than me, broader than me... uglier than me. Every now and then, he'll cast a not-so-subtle glance in my direction. He doesn't attempt to communicate or kill me, but it's not hard to miss the disdain in his eyes.

As the only American here, I feel a little conspicuous.

I vaguely recognize one of the tattoos on his right forearm as that of a well-established Russian mob family. His peers hold him in high regard. The symbol I can see signifies his rank, and he's right up there.

One slightly positive thing is that he's not a member of the same family as my target. The guy I'm in here to kill is Yuri... something. I don't know. It had a lot of Ks and Zs and Vs in it, and simply calling him Yuri is easier. He's a lieutenant in the Khaliskov gang and the right-hand man to the guy who runs it. My client, Petrov, is the right-hand man to the leader of a rival organization, the Vikslavich family. Fedorov is a member of a third gang, the Rahzva. Those three are the big players in Russian organized crime. Now, I have no desire to get involved in the politics of it all, but I'm fairly sure me killing one of them on behalf of another will start a war. I just hope Petrov is true to his word and gets me out of here before it all goes to shit.

I sigh. I'm hungry. We've just had thirty minutes to walk around outside. Compulsory exercise, I'm guessing. Dinner will be in about an hour or so, I think. That's if my internal clock is still working. I don't feel I can trust it anymore. It's not that this place is getting inside my head—not yet anyway, although I'm fully aware that's a danger, the longer I stay here. It's more that I'm feeling... disoriented. I never knew how effective removing someone's sense of time could be. I'm using my hunger as a gauge for what time it is, which is far from ideal.

I sigh again. I'm not exactly the patient type. It's killing me having to sit here and—

Uh-oh.

Fedorov has stopped pacing. Now, he's just... staring at

me. His eyes are piercing and dark. He has short hair but a long beard.

I haven't had much experience being in prison. I've watched a few movies set in a prison, but that probably doesn't count. Still, my mantra of antagonizing anyone who tries to give me shit should work anywhere, right?

I raise an eyebrow. "Is there a problem, Captain Smirnoff?"

He takes a deep breath, which swells his chest and broadens his shoulders. He looks angry. I'm pretty sure I haven't done anything except sit here. How can *that* piss someone off?

I swing my legs over the side of the bed and shrug my blanket from my shoulders. I stand but don't move toward him. "What?"

Fedorov smirks, which makes him look arrogant. He says something...

...

...

...

Nope, didn't catch any of it.

I shake my head. "Sorry, I don't speak Communist. Can you repeat that in a real language, please?"

He looks even angrier now, so I know he can understand me. He's just speaking Russian to get under my skin. He's posturing. He's done it a few times since I got here. He's not making any move toward me, so it doesn't appear he wants to engage. Maybe he's just doing it to entertain himself?

Well, screw it. I'm bored too.

I take a step toward him. It's not the largest of cells to begin with, and now we're only a couple of feet apart. There's no denying he's physically bigger than me, despite us both being roughly the same height. And his beard is better than mine.

I hold his gaze, unblinking and unafraid. If he makes one move that I deem threatening, I'll kill him where he stands. He's not part of the job, but in a place like this, only the strong survive. It won't do me any harm to send a message to everyone else.

Do not fuck with the American.

Neither of us is backing down. It's been maybe twenty seconds... thirty. It's pretty intense, but I'm not—

Fedorov smirks again and turns away. He takes a small step away from me and resumes his pacing, completely ignoring me. I watch him for a moment, then sit back down on my bed, wrap my blankets around me, and lean against the wall once more.

Damn right.

Prick.

2

??:??

The cell door clicks and slowly starts to roll open. Very little light is shining through the sorry excuse for a window now. I stand, stretch, and crack my neck and shoulders. I'm not sure exactly how much time has passed. It's probably been twenty minutes but feels like two weeks.

Still... time to eat.

I move toward the door, but Fedorov pushes in front of me and steps out first.

I clench my jaw muscles repeatedly, fighting the urge to slam his head into the nearest wall until it bursts open like a watermelon.

I count to five and relax. It's not a fight worth having. It's not a victory over me, and it doesn't matter to me if he thinks it is. I follow him out and fall in line with everyone else.

The prison has three cell blocks, each stretching out from a central hub. The number is written on the wall above the main set of doors. I don't have any clue about the Russian language, but mine has a small O and a mirrored N in it, so I'm guessing it's cell block one. I might be wrong, but I don't really care.

The block is a large, rectangular space, with parallel rows of cells spread over two floors, running the full width of the enclosure. Two sets of stairs in the middle lead up to the metal gantry running around the edge of the upper rows, which I'm currently standing on. All the prisoners are filing out, shuffling uncomfortably toward the stairs.

There's a line of armed guards below me, keeping an eye on everyone. You've got to be a crazy kind of tough to work in a place like this. They won't take any shit, regardless of which crime family you're a part of. I think the inmates respect that too. There's the usual amount of shoving and insults, but no one's stepping out of line.

I make my way slowly down the stairs, merging with the line of prisoners from the first floor. There's some more shoving but nothing intense. The guard shouts something, and everyone falls silent. I have no clue what they're saying, so I just do what everyone else does.

The door at the end slides open, and the line of inmates is ushered through. It's a short walk along a narrow corridor. The walls are exposed brick and offer no insulation against the elements outside. The floor is concrete, cracked, and covered with damp patches. Our collective footsteps echo ominously as we make our way to the canteen.

I've been here a few times now, and the closest comparison I can draw is that of feeding time at the zoo. Except the animals probably get better food. All three cell blocks enter at the same time from three different doors. It's then an organized scramble to get in line by the serving hatch, so they can throw some regurgitated rice and beans onto a plate for you. Cold rice and beans, I might add. You then have to find a seat that's not with the wrong group of people. Which, in my case, is everyone.

We enter the canteen. Our line is nearest to the hatch, so we'll be eating first. I scan the huge crowd with an absent curiosity as I wait, holding a plastic tray with sections molded into it for the food.

There's another gantry looking down at the large room, with multiple armed guards keeping watch over us all. There are more guards pacing menacingly around the room, just looking for a reason to beat someone.

The other cell blocks are grouping together, joining the line we've started. I shuffle closer to the hatch. My stomach rumbles, though it's out of necessity rather than excitement. My last few meals have been... dubious, to say the least. The first day, I got—

Oh, hello... what have we here?

A group of three inmates has just walked past me, heading for the front of the line. They're trying to push in a few places ahead of me. The low murmur of conversation is getting louder, and the shoving and posturing is getting more intense.

Whoever those three are, they're brave bastards.

There's more commotion ahead of me, and the shouting is getting louder, sounding more aggressive. I peer around the guy standing directly in front of me and look at what's happening.

The three guys who cut in have just been unceremoniously shoved out of the line. People are gesturing with their hands, which I'm guessing is their way of telling them to get to the back of the line.

I roll my eyes. I never understood the need to prove yourself to everyone. *Hey, look at me. Look how tough I am.*

Give me a break. All it does is make you look like an asshole. These three being a prime example. I don't recognize any of them, so I'm not sure which block they're from. Or which—

Ah, shit.

Rookie error, Adrian.

I let my gaze wander, and I've just caught myself staring at them. Unfortunately, they've just caught me staring at them too, and now they're making their way toward me.

Double shit.

I know how this works. It's the same anywhere you go, prison or otherwise. If someone tries to act like the top dog and gets put in their place, the first thing they do is target someone weaker to quickly mend any damage to their reputation.

And the three Russian stooges here clearly think I'm the one to target.

They all look the same—tall, tattooed, pissed off... and all staring a hole right through me. The problem I have, despite knowing I'm *definitely* on my own in what's about to happen, is that I don't know which family they're associated with. Regardless of why I'm here, this whole place is a goddamn time bomb waiting to go off. It's as political as it is violent. If I take these three out and they're affiliated with my employer, I run the risk of losing my way out of here, even if I do manage to carry out the hit.

But I can't just let them attack me.

The people on either side of me in the line step away, creating a large space for these three assholes to fill. They stop a few feet away, in a loose semicircle. Silence has fallen. I look up at the gantry and see the guards aren't paying attention. Even the people who threw them out of the line are looking on, bemused.

It seems nothing unites rival Russian gangs more than the universal hatred for an American.

Where was I up to? Oh, yeah... *triple* shit.

I hold my empty tray in both hands and move one leg back slightly, dropping into a loose stance, ready to move. Everyone's watching. This is the perfect time to make a statement, to show people I'm not one to mess with, but I don't want to piss off the people who can get me out of here.

Think, Adrian... think!

The guy in the middle steps forward. He smiles, revealing his blackened, rotten teeth. He flicks his tongue out at me like a snake. "American. You got problem?"

It appears my next move has been determined for me. Only one thing to do, I guess.

I shrug. "Technically, I've got three."

He frowns. "You think you're funny?"

"I do, yeah. Do you think you're intimidating?"

He nods slowly, grinning. "I do."

"Well, one of us is wrong, pal. And let me tell you, I'm a hit at dinner parties, so..."

"I'm going to crush your tiny head, American. Then you will respect Rahzva."

Did he say Rahzva?

Oh, thank God. The only person I'm going to piss off by wiping the floor with these three pricks is my cellmate, and if he says anything, I'll kick his ass too.

I relax my stance and stand tall. "Oh, I respect *Rahzva*. I just think you, personally, are a dick."

His eyes grow wide, and he raises both hands, fists clenched. I notice a thick, gold ring on his left hand. I didn't think jewelry was allowed in prison. Although, it's not surprising that a few of the rules are bent or ignored in a place like this. That'll sting if it hits me...

I quickly assess his body language. A glance up and down is all I need. He's dropping his weight slightly to his left, which means a strong left hand is about to come flying toward my head.

I tense my arms, ready to defend myself. I don't think this guy's going to wait for his friends to do or say anything. This isn't the type of place where you rely on anyone, even those who have your back.

I take a deep breath and feel time slowing down around me. It's a skill I've honed over many years, and along with my fast reflexes, it allows me to see any situation objectively. It's almost as if I'm reacting to something that hasn't happened.

I take a step toward him. I bring the tray up in one hand and whip it forward like a Frisbee, slicing it into his throat before he can throw his punch.

What's that saying? Do unto others before they do unto you?

Something like that.

Anyway, all that gentlemanly crap will get you killed in a place like this. You hit first and hit harder, end of story.

His eyes pop wide, and he sinks to his knees, clutching his throat. His breathing is uncomfortably loud and coming in quick rasps. I hit him with a good shot. If I'm lucky, I might have damaged his trachea. It certainly sounds like it.

I take the tray in both hands and swing it hard into the side of his head. It snaps in two as it crashes against the guy's temple. He slumps sideways and hits the floor, unconscious. I drop the half of the tray I'm still holding next to him and look at the guy's two friends. They're standing still, their mouths hanging open in shock. I glance around the room. Everyone else is doing pretty much the same.

I raise my hands in a loose fighting stance. "Who's next?"

They exchange a look, and their expressions fade from surprise to anger. They yell something guttural and Russian, then charge at me in tandem.

Oh, boy...

The guy on my left will reach me first, so he's next. He throws a punch at full speed. It's well timed but too easy to telegraph. I bring my arm up, bent, to cover my head. His punch connects on the point of my elbow. It sends a dull pain shooting up and down my arm, but it's nothing compared to what he'll be feeling right now. The elbow is a tough, thick bone, and when it's bent, the whole thing is like a brick. And this guy has just punched it really hard.

He screams out, likely because every bone in his hand has just shattered. As he stands off, I instinctively roll under the potential follow-up punch and push through with a punch that's half-hook, half-uppercut. It lands on his exposed jaw, and his head snaps back under the impact. I'm not sure if he's out cold, but he's on the floor, which will do.

As I turn to face the remaining guy, I step through and launch a kick that could score a forty-yard field goal. It connects perfectly with his balls as he's running and practically takes him off his feet. He staggers away from me, toward the serving counter, so I reach for him and grab two handfuls of his jumpsuit. I pull him toward me, lowering my head slightly and pushing it forward as I do. The head-butt smashes into his oncoming face, and I feel the instant warmth of blood as his nose explodes. I sling him around, tossing him to the floor next to his friends.

I'm breathing heavily, not even trying to keep the rush of adrenaline at bay. After four days of being stuck here, I finally get to let out some of my aggression and frustration. My teeth are aching from tensing my jaw so hard. I repeatedly clench my fists as I look around the stunned, silent cafeteria, desperate for another fight.

My mind is... conflicted at times. I'm not crazy; I just have some issues I'm still working on. What can I tell you? It's been a rough few years. See, I typically have two voices in my head, which tend to balance each other out in most situations. One of them, which is the closest thing to reason, is telling me it's not healthy to feel so alive after imposing so much violence, and I need to step down before things get out of hand. But the other voice, which I like to call my Inner Satan, is telling me to continue the slaughter and send a message to everyone, to let them know I'm not one with whom to fuck. I usually live in the middle ground between the two, but right now, my Inner Satan is shouting louder.

"Come on! Who's next?" I yell.

No one moves. Seconds tick by in the eerie silence. A whistle blows somewhere off to my right. The sound of bustling activity fills the air as everyone moves as one, first stepping back to the wall, then dropping to one knee. I stand still, watching the disciplined movements of every prisoner.

Doors are thrust open on both sides, slamming loudly against the walls. Armed guards dressed in riot gear storm in, surrounding me. The mechanical crunching of guns sounds out on the gantry above me. A small team of three appears in front of me, screaming something I don't understand. They're gesturing wildly with their hands, so I assume they want me on my knees, like everyone else.

Slowly, my breathing slows, and the rush of adrenaline-fueled anger begins to fade. I lower myself to the floor, holding my arms out wide, with my palms facing the guards.

"They started it," I say, knowing it's wasted breath.

The three guards rush me, pinning me to the floor on my front. They roughly secure my hands behind my back and haul me upright to my feet. As two of them hold me, one moves in front, standing so that his face is merely inches from mine. He smiles, displaying yellow, rotten teeth.

Uh!

Ah!

He just jabbed me twice with a nightstick, once in the gut, once in the side, just below my ribs. I try to keel over, but they hold me still. I take deep breaths, trying to ignore the pain. The guy in front grabs my chin and holds my face up to his. He says something I don't understand. His tone was harsh, and he practically spat the words out, so I'm guessing it was something insulting.

They frog-march me toward the door leading back to my cell block. I try to look around as best I can. Most people are looking, though only a couple don't have a look of surprise on their faces. No sign of my target, Yuri, either. I wonder where he is.

We're heading back along the corridor. The low murmuring of conversation has resumed behind me and is fading quickly from earshot. Without the other prisoners around me, it's even colder in here now. I can see my breath in front of me.

The team of three has formed a loose triangle around me, and they're guiding me back up the stairs to my cell. We stop outside it, and two men move to either side of the doorway. The third guy, with the yellow teeth, spins me around and takes the restraints off my wrists. He pushes me inside, then mutters something into the radio he has pinned to his chest. A familiar whirring noise ramps up, and the cell door rolls shut.

I watch the guards walk away, then sit on my bed, wrap

the blankets around me, and lean back against the wall. I let out a heavy sigh, wincing as a sharp pain in my chest reminds me of the nightstick that was recently shoved into my ribs.

Goddammit.

I didn't even get to eat...

3

??:??

I can hear multiple footsteps outside my cell, growing louder every second. I reckon it's been a good half-hour since I was escorted back here, so I'm guessing dinnertime is over.

Yeah, the guards are shouting now.

I'm so hungry. The hardest part of this job isn't giving up warmth, sleep, or freedom. It's giving up a decent meal. Coupled with my outstanding lack of patience and reasonably short temper, it's safe to say I'm not doing so well right now. I just need to—

Fedorov has just appeared in the doorway. Man, he looks pissed. More so than usual, I mean. Probably because I just kicked the shit out of three of his buddies.

Well, *this* isn't awkward...

I don't bother moving. He won't do anything when all the guards are walking around. He's still glaring at me, but he walks over to his bunk and sits down without a word. A moment later, a guard walks past and glances inside, performing his routine check before the door's locked. He looks at me for a second longer than normal, then disappears.

I imagine I'm the topic of most people's conversations in here now, which certainly won't help me keep a low profile. I have to find a way to—

Oh, Christ... what now?

Someone else has appeared in the doorway, flanked by two more guys behind him. He's shorter than me but not short. His hair is long enough to start curling around the edges, giving him that trendy, scruffy look. But he looks old enough that fashion shouldn't matter too much to him.

He throws a look at my cellmate, who gets to his feet and starts shifting uncomfortably on the spot. The guy at the door gestures with his thumb and says something to him in Russian. He seems reluctant to reply. He keeps switching his gaze between me and the people at the door.

The guy at the door repeats whatever he just said, only a little louder. This time, my cellmate walks outside, turning his body to squeeze between the two guys guarding the entrance. He disappears out of sight, leaving me alone with my visitor.

The guy looks at me and smiles. "American."

I adjust my position, bringing one knee up to my chest so that I can rest my arm on it. I smile back. "That's me. Like apple pie and Cadillacs. And you are?"

"I am Vladimir."

"Okay..."

"I speak with Petrov. Told him about fight."

I nod. "Ah, I see. So, you and your friends are Vikslavich?"

"We are. Petrov is not happy about attention you get."

I shrug. "Neither am I. I didn't ask for those three assholes to pick a fight with me. I had to defend myself, and in doing so, I missed out on a meal. Believe me, I'm more pissed off about all this than Petrov is."

Vladimir paces back and forth, then stands beside the bed opposite. He makes a point of dusting it with his hand before sitting down. He fiddles with his hands, cracking his knuckles. "It is... regrettable, yes, but not our problem. We have... amendments to your contract."

Huh?

I sit up, swing my legs over the side, and shake my head. "You can't change the terms. I'm here, I was paid upfront, and I'll do the job. I'm the best there is. Petrov wouldn't have hired me if he didn't believe that. So, let me do what I'm good at, and trust I'll deliver."

Vladimir shakes his head. "Your skills are not problem. Time is problem. Your little skirmish before has caused... ruckus. So, we must change our plans."

I don't like the sound of this.

"Change them to what, exactly?"

He stands. "We want Yuri dead by morning. And you frame Rahzva dogs for his death."

I frown. "Hey, wait a minute. Shit like that takes time and planning. You can't just—"

He walks over to the door, then turns to face me. "You have until sunrise."

I sigh. "And if I can't pull it off?"

He shrugs. "Then our offer to get you out of here... expires."

Vladimir walks out, and his two men disappear with him. A few moments later, the guard who walked by before reappears, followed by my cellmate. He steps back inside and sits down on his bed. The guard looks at me, not taking his eyes off mine as the door rolls shut. He walks away as the lock clicks.

Great.

Now what do I do?

4

It's well into dusk outside now. Unbelievably, the temperature drops at night. I didn't think it could get any colder! I absently run my hand over the brick of the outside wall, feeling the icy grasp of the unforgiving weather beyond.

I'm pacing around the cell, trying to figure out how the hell am I meant to kill Yuri before sunrise when we're locked down for the night? And frame Rahzva? I know I'm good, but this is impossible!

Federov is lying on his bunk, staring up at the ceiling, cracking his knuckles repeatedly. I sigh heavily, which prompts him to look over at me. I meet his gaze, and he sneers, muttering something under his breath. I probably wouldn't understand it even if I could make it out.

Man, I want to break that guy's face.

I raise my eyebrow.

Wait a minute...

229

Hang on... it's coming...

Almost got it...

There it is!

Lightbulb!

I know exactly how I'm going to kill Yuri and frame the Rahzva for it.

Damn, I'm good.

I move over to the door and press my face against the bars, trying to see down to the left. There are two ways in and out of the cell block. The door on the right leads to the canteen, but the door to the left leads out to the main network of corridors and the security station that oversees all three cell blocks. I'm waiting for the guards to come in and perform their last cell check of the day. They won't open the doors, but they do a walk-by.

I hear the click of the lock below me. From this angle, I can just about see the corner of the door when it's open. Yeah, I just saw it swing into view.

Here they come.

Showtime.

I hope this works. I'm probably dead if it doesn't, so... no pressure.

I turn around and stare openly at Fedorov. "Hey, asshole."

His head moves slightly, and we lock eyes. There's no expression on his face. He breathes deeply but says nothing.

I smile. "I'm talking to you, you ugly bastard. Why don't you mutter something else under your breath about me? Fucking coward..."

He slowly sits up, placing both hands on the edge of the bed. He never breaks eye contact.

"I know you can understand me, prick. So, understand

this—wanna know how I was caught? They walked in on me slipping one to your sister."

He's on his feet in an instant, snarling and spitting, glaring with wide, angry eyes.

Yeah, that did it!

Fedorov charges toward me head-on, which is evidence that he's not thinking clearly. If you do that in an enclosed space, it limits your options for movement and makes you an easy counter-target. But it appears he's so overcome with rage, he doesn't care about such trivialities, which means I've done my job right.

He says something as he closes in and raises his right arm, presumably to throw a punch. I'm only a couple of inches from the bars. I need to let him have a shot at me. I'm fighting every natural urge to move. I get my arms up just as he connects.

Uh!

Shit... that hurt!

I'm forced back against the bars from the impact. I quickly move a hand to my nose. I feel the warm trickle of blood.

That will do nicely.

Right.

Fedorov winds up another shot, but I duck and roll under his arm. I throw a stiff jab to the side of his ribs as I sidestep away, positioning myself behind him. His follow-up hits thin air. He exhales heavily, resting against the cell door, holding his side.

I can't give him even a second to rest.

I use both hands and slam his head into the wall at the foot of my bunk with as much force as I can. It makes a dull, sickening thud, and he stands, dazed. I put my hands on the back of his head and ram his face forward a second time.

And a third. And a fourth. Each time, the impact sounds wetter, and after that last one, his face is a bloody mess. His nose is all kinds of busted, and his lip is split.

I've been dying to do that for days! Man, it felt good.

Anyway...

He's barely conscious, so I grab a handful of his collar and throw him onto his bunk. I quickly pat him down.

Come on... you must have something...

Shit.

No contraband.

What kind of prisoner doesn't have any—

Hang on.

I raise his left arm and take a closer look at his hand.

What have we here? Fedorov's wearing a ring on his middle finger. It's gold and chunky, with a raised symbol of a cross on it. I saw the exact same ring on the guy in the canteen earlier. I didn't think anything of it at the time, but if this guy has one too, I'm guessing it's some sort of coat-of-arms for the Rahzva.

Perfect! I slide it off his finger and put it on my pocket for later.

Now... the fun part.

I move over to the bars and start banging on them as loud as I can, slamming my palms against them repeatedly until they sting. "Hey! Hey, guards! My cellmate's gone crazy! He's attacked me! Guards!"

There's one walking just below my cell. I recognize him. His name's Angeloff. He steps back, so he can see past the gantry, and stares at me. He shouts something, then carries on walking.

Shit.

"Hey, asshole! Look at me! He hit me and then started

bashing his head against the wall! He's lost it, man, I'm telling you! You gotta get some medical attention up here!"

Angeloff stops in his tracks and looks over his shoulder, back up at me. He sighs, then calls to one of his colleagues who is standing just out of view. I can hear their footsteps on the metal stairs of the gantry, just to the right of my cell.

Here they come.

I step back from the cell door as I hear them approach. They stop in front of me, and Angeloff stares at me wearily. I gesture to the other bunk. His gaze flicks past me. A second later, his eyes pop wide.

He shouts something over his shoulder, and a moment later, my cell door opens. The other guard rushes to my cellmate. Angeloff walks in behind him, glances over at the bed, then stops in front of me.

"What happened?" he asks.

I shrug. "It's like I said. He went nuts, hit me..." I pause to point at my bloodied nose. "Then he started headbutting the wall until he knocked himself out. He was mumbling something, but I didn't understand him. I got him onto his bunk, and then shouted for help."

Angeloff's eyes narrow. I think he might be a senior guard. His uniform looks cleaner than the other guy's. He's standing taller too. Not that he's *actually* taller, but his shoulders are back, and his chest is a little puffed out, as if he's stood to attention.

"He just... went crazy?"

I nod.

"I find that hard to believe, American. This man has shown no signs of mental distress during his time here."

I shrug again. "What can I say? He wouldn't be the first person who couldn't stand living with me."

Angeloff looks over at his colleague, says something to him in Russian, and then turns to leave.

I take a deep breath. Now for the risky part.

I step toward Angeloff and grab his arm. He snaps his head around and looks at me as if I just took a shit on his pillow. "What the fuck are you doing? You have a death wish, American?"

I smile. "Like you wouldn't believe..."

Still holding onto him, I take a swing with my left and catch him on the side of the face. I didn't put too much behind it. I don't want to seriously hurt the guy. I'm just doing enough to serve a purpose.

His colleague tackles me and wrestles me to the floor. I land awkwardly on my shoulder, but I resist the urge to fight him. He blows his whistle while leaning right next to my ear, which is *really* fucking loud! Damn it! It takes a couple of moments for the ringing to subside. Once it has, I can hear the rapid stomping of boots coming from below. Less than thirty seconds later, there are four more guards piling inside my cell, desperate to help pin me down.

Well, I think it worked!

They're all shouting at me, talking over each other. I doubt I could understand them even if I knew the language. They haul me to my feet and spread out as much as the small cell allows them to. I have a guard on either side of me, each holding me in place by my arms, and another behind me, with his arm wrapped around my neck. Angeloff moves in front of me. His nostrils flare with anger as he glares at me through a deep frown. His eyebrows are bushy and flecked with gray.

Uh!

He just rammed his nightstick into my gut.

Yeah... fair enough. I guess you could argue I deserved that. I mean—

Uh!

He just hit me again. I breathe deeply through the pain. Okay, I think *two* is a bit much!

"I think you are the crazy one, American," he says, spitting as he talks. "Maybe a day in The Hole will make you see sense, no?"

I roll my eyes. While this is all part of my plan... sort of... if you can call it that... the prospect of being shoved inside a five-by-five room with no windows, no light, no bed, and no food for twenty-four hours doesn't really appeal to me.

I'm frog-marched out of my cell and down the stairs. I don't fight it. I just try to make eye contact with as many prisoners as I can on my way past.

I shout, "You wanna see crazy? Do you? I'll show you fucking crazy! Let's tear this place down! Kill them all!"

The noise is growing around me. Prisoners on both floors are shouting, banging their hands against their cell doors. It doesn't take much to fire the inmates up. They're all tough, bored, and angry. Any reason to fight is a good one.

More guards appear, rushing past me as I'm escorted out of the block through the left door. On the other side, away from the cells, is a small network of corridors. I get the feeling this whole prison is one of those places the Russian government isn't in a rush to admit exists. Clearly, funding for it is kept to a bare minimum. The floor is exposed concrete, once smooth, now stained with damp. The rooms aren't really rooms; they're just sections shaped by false walls, with no ceilings.

The rebellious commotion fades away as we walk farther along the main corridor. It's awkward moving with Angeloff and his friends surrounding me. Luckily, they won't be for long. The corridor splits just ahead of us, and I can see the room I'm looking for on the left. As we approach it, I look inside and note the position of the two guards— one sitting at a computer terminal, the other stood with his back to him, talking into his radio.

The control room.

As we draw level, I run through my next few moves in my head, making sure I know what I'm doing and what could go wrong, so I'm prepared. The three guards with me are all armed, but their guns are holstered and fastened in, which is a rookie error. Still, I'm not complaining, as it means I'm far less likely to be shot when I do *this*...

I whip my head back, slamming it into the face of the guy behind me. A dull pain explodes around the base of my skull. I didn't get the angle quite right, and I think I hit his forehead. Granted, it would've hurt him a lot more than it hurt me, but it still sucks.

He releases his grip a split-second after the impact, allowing me to move more freely. The guards on either side of me both have a firm, one-handed grip of my arms, just above my elbow. I circle my arms up and back, twisting free of their clutches, then grab their wrists in my hands. I quickly drop to the floor, pulling my arms together as I do. The guards are stunned and are dragged toward each other. I let go as they collide and roll backward as they crash to the floor.

I use my own momentum to roll back through and up onto my feet. I'm now standing a few paces away from where I was, level with the guy I headbutted a few moments ago. I drop to one knee and smash my elbow down into his face, just as he tries to sit up. His body sags as consciousness leaves him.

I spring to my feet and rush toward the others, who

seem to be coming to their senses a little. I throw a low, hard kick at the guy on the left, which connects on the outside of the leg, just below the knee. He topples over, and I step into him, slamming my fist into his temple as he falls.

I don't wait to see if he hits the floor. I know that's a given after that punch. I spin clockwise and throw the same fist into the last guy's gut. He grunts from the blow. As he's keeling over, I place my other hand on the back of his head and bring my knee up, fast and hard, into his face. He crumples to the floor, down for the count and probably with a busted nose.

I crouch beside him and take his pistol. It's a Makarov. Not a bad weapon, but I would never choose to use it. It's too small and delicate. I feel as if I'm about to break the damn thing. My weapon of choice is a Beretta, which is a little bulkier, but the size and weight gives me comfort and feels more reliable in my hand.

I can tell by the weight that it's carrying a full mag, so I don't check it. I don't have much time. I run around the corner and into the control room. The two guards look at me, their faces frozen with shock, unable to comprehend why a prisoner is standing in front of them.

I ignore the guy sitting down for now. By the time he's pushed himself away from the desk and onto his feet, it'll be too late. I step quickly toward the guard standing up and slam the butt of the pistol into his face. His eyes roll back in his head, and he falls dramatically backward, crashing into a file cabinet before hitting the floor.

What a pussy! I barely touched him. And these are the guys keeping all the imprisoned members of the Russian mafia in check? Jesus...

I spin around and point the Makarov unwaveringly at the last guard's forehead. He snaps his hands up, palms open, and shakes his head. He mutters something hurriedly, which I'm going to assume was something along the lines of *Don't shoot me.* I grab his collar and drag him from his chair. He sprawls to the floor. I move over to him and slam my boot into the side of his head.

I look around outside. No alarms, no more guards. They're all too busy calming down the residents of cell block one, hopefully. I sigh with relief.

So far, so good.

I sit down at the computer terminal. This is the kind of thing Josh excels at, but I'll give it a go. I just need to figure out—

Oh.

Shit.

Shit. Damn it. Shit. Shit.

Everything's in Russian!

5

??:??

Okay, Adrian... think! I'll have to use one of the guards—no other way around it. Who is the least unconscious? I stand and look out through the window at the three I left lying in the corridor. None of them have moved.

I hear a groaning to my right and snap my head around. The guard near the file cabinets is stirring. He'll do.

I pace over to him and grab a handful of his collar. I lift him up to his knees and place the barrel of the gun against his cheek. "Do you speak English?"

He nods hurriedly.

"Good. I need you to do something for me." I drag him over to the console and shove him unceremoniously into the chair. I keep the gun on him and point to the screen. "I need you to bring up a list of every prisoner in here. I'm looking for someone."

He nods again. "D-do not shoot me."

"Do what I ask, and I won't."

He taps a few keys, and the screen flickers as a huge list loads up. The guard gestures to it. "There. Who is it you are looking for?"

I frown. "Yuri... something. Begins with a K."

He swallows hard, and a bead of sweat forms almost instantly on his brow. I can hear his breathing getting a little faster, and his eyes are wide. I know fear when I see it. He must know exactly who I'm looking for.

"You know who I mean?"

He nods. "Yes."

"Where is he?"

He glances sideways at me, hesitating. His fingers hover over the keys, frozen with reluctance.

I push the barrel hard against the side of his head. "Considering you don't want to get shot, you're doing a good job of pissing me off."

He starts to sob but stops himself, breathing as if he's meditating or trying to stop a panic attack. "He... he... he will kill you. Why do you—"

"Let me worry about that. Just tell me where he is."

He points at the screen. "There."

I look at the word, but it means nothing.

"What's that?"

The guard holds up two fingers, like a peace sign.

"Oh, he's in cell block two? Is that what it says?"

The guard nods.

"Thank you. See? That wasn't so hard, was it? Now, there's one last, tiny, little thing I need you to do."

His shoulders slump forward. "What?"

"I'm gonna need you to open every cell door in all three blocks."

The guard widens his eyes to the point where I'm concerned they might just... fall out of their sockets. He turns his head slowly to look up at me. "I can't... I... I can't—"

"Sure, you can... ah..." I lean forward, trying to see his nametag, but it's illegible. "Screw it, I'm just gonna call you Bob. Sure, you can, *Bob*. Same way you unlock them all when it's time to eat."

He's practically hyperventilating. "No... I... We have men in all three blocks... If I... They would..."

I pat him on his shoulder. "All valid points, I'm sure. But I gotta tell you, Bob, if I had two shits, I still wouldn't give 'em. Do you understand what I'm saying? Now, open... the cell... doors."

He presses a few buttons, and I hear a loud buzz, followed by a familiar click.

There they go. The caged animals are free to roam the zoo. Let's hope they take the bait.

I smile. "Thanks a lot, Bob. Don't think I don't appreciate your help because I do."

In a swift movement, I slam the butt of the pistol against his head, and he slumps forward, sprawled over the keyboard.

"What a guy..."

I sprint out into the corridor and stop beside another of the fallen guards. I take his pistol, chamber a round, and stand, holding a gun in each hand.

I close my eyes. Take a deep breath. And another. Then I open them again.

Game time.

I sprint forward, rushing back along the corridor to my cell block. I'm only halfway there, and the noise is intense. Sounds like...

I slide to a stop in the doorway, stunned by the scene before me.

...a full-scale riot.

Holy shit!

The air is filled with shouting and screaming. It's complete carnage. Prisoners are running everywhere, without any immediately obvious purpose. The guards are huddled together in a small circle in the center of the block, surrounded by a mass of inmates. I can just about see five of them, all waving their guns in shaking hands.

Not the type of crowd that intimidates easily.

Normally, I would feel bad for the guards. But in this place, they're just as bad as the prisoners, so screw them. I set off running again. I need to navigate this chaos and make my way to the other cell block. I just need to avoid—

Uh-oh.

Three guys are heading toward me. They look mad.

Well, I don't have time for this. It won't be long before reinforcements storm the place, dressed in riot gear, and take control.

I don't slow down. I don't even break stride. I raise both arms and fire both guns. I clip all three of them at least twice, sending them sprawling to the floor, dead. A few people look around, but it doesn't seem to deter anyone.

I dodge, jump, and duck my way through the crowd and make it to the far end. I head through the door, toward the canteen. There are two more inmates ahead of me, whom I don't immediately recognize. They must be from another cell block.

Wrong day to get in my way, fellas.

I raise both guns again and put a bullet through each of their foreheads. They drop like stones as I sprint past them into the canteen. As I enter, there's a door ahead of me and one away to the left, which lead to the other cell blocks. That guard back there said Yuri is in block two, and the layout on the screen showed that's through the left door. I head in that direction, avoiding the small groups of inmates gathered here. Thankfully, they aren't paying me too much attention.

I'm breathing heavily. The temperature and my incarceration over the last few days has done nothing for my fitness. But I can't worry about that now. I've got a job to do and a very short amount of time to do it.

I emerge at full speed into cell block two and slide to a stop before anyone notices me. It looks a lot like mine in here. Prisoners are everywhere, guards' bodies are strewn across the floor, and the noise sounds like a football stadium. I discard the guns. I don't want to be caught with them on me, and having them makes me a beacon among the other inmates.

This is the hardest part. I know what Yuri looks like, but I haven't actually seen him since I got here. I slowly navigate the crowds, pausing occasionally to punch someone, so it looks as if I'm joining in. No one's made a point of attacking me directly, which I'm hoping is a sign that people are less interested in the American on this side.

If I were a high-ranking Russian mafia lieutenant, where would I be in a riot?

I smile. I'd be in my cell because I'd be smart enough not to risk adding time onto my sentence.

I start looking side to side, checking every cell I pass to see if I'm right.

No.

No.

Damn it.

No.

No.

Shit. I'm almost at the end of the block, and there's no

sign of him. Which means, assuming I'm right, he's on the upper level.

I take a deep breath to steel myself and turn around to head back to the stairs. A guy jumps in front of me, his arms raised, growling as he bares his teeth like an animal.

What the...

I kick the front of his knee, pushing my foot forward and down. The joint is forced back against itself. With all his weight on it, it snaps like a twig. His snarl turns to shock; his eyes bulge, and his stunned silence is likely the only thing stopping him from screaming.

He crumbles to the floor, clutching his leg. I look down at him as I step past. "Move, asshole."

I make it to the stairs. I'll head left first. When in doubt, go left—it's one of the rules I live by. I push my way up and head left along the gantry, checking the cells.

No.

No.

No.

Bingo.

Yuri's sitting alone in his cell, resting against the wall, calmly reading a book. He looks up as I move inside and frowns when he doesn't recognize me. I slip my hand inside my pocket, fumbling around until Fedorov's ring is on my finger.

I smile. "Hello, Yuri."

Before he can move, I lunge at him, grab his throat, and pin him to the wall. He grabs my wrist with both hands, pushing back to try to alleviate some of the pressure, but it's not working. I have all my weight against him and the advantage from standing.

He has no chance.

In a few seconds, I'm going to crush his larynx, and he'll essentially suffocate. But first...

I raise my other hand and clench my fist, exposing the ring on my finger.

"Nothing... personal..." I say through gritted teeth.

I hit him in the face. Once, twice, repeatedly—smashing him over and again. I make sure to hit his forehead a few times. It won't hurt him as much, but it serves a purpose.

I rain down blows on his face with a relentless fury. Almost a week's worth of pent-up frustration is unleashed in under a minute. He's not defending himself because he's focusing on trying to move my other hand from around his throat. His face is contorted with the struggle and is slowly turning into a crimson mask. I feel his cheek split, his nose explode, his jaw dislocate...

Finally, his grip loosens.

He's done.

I step away and quickly wipe the blood from my hands on his bedsheets before it dries and stains the skin. I slip the ring off my finger, back into my pocket, and then walk out of the cell. I force myself to keep a discreet pace as I make my way back down the stairs, toward the door that leads to the canteen. I blend in with the chaotic backdrop and make it into the corridor without further incident.

Now, I run.

I sprint as if there's a gold medal waiting for me. Through the canteen, back along the corridor, and into my own cell block. The scene hasn't changed much. There are fewer guards than before, but the prisoners are still enjoying their moment of freedom.

I take the stairs two at a time, back up to my cell. My roommate is still lying unconscious on his bed. The guard who was tending to him has long gone. I slide the ring back onto his finger, then head back outside. I make my way down the stairs and wait. I look around, taking deep breaths to slow my heart rate and help the adrenaline subside. A strange calm washes over me. A type of serenity that has no business in a place like this.

I caused all of this.

You have to be a little impressed. It's been... what? Half an hour since I smashed my cellmate's face into the wall? In that time, I've single-handedly orchestrated a prison riot, taken out a half-dozen guards, and carried out an intricate assassination with little time to plan it.

Not bad.

But now... now comes the shitty part. Now, I wait.

6
_____

??:??

I have no clue how long I've been in here. The Hole is just…
awful. I can't stand up because the ceiling isn't high enough,
and I can't lie down fully because it's not wide enough.

If I were to guess, I would say I've been in here a day.
Maybe two. After I stepped outside my cell, it was only a few
minutes until the riot team arrived. Tear gas canisters were
launched in all directions, prompting the inmates—me
included—to drop to the floor. A swarm of guards dressed
in riot gear stormed in. It took them about twenty seconds to
locate me, drag me to my feet, and haul me away. They
threw me in this room and slammed the door shut
behind me.

I've had my eyes closed pretty much since the moment
they threw me in here. I wasn't meditating. I was simply
trying to talk myself out of thinking how hungry and tired
I am.

The door opens, and the sudden influx of light stings my

eyes, forcing me to squint. A blurry outline stands before me. "On your feet."

I don't recognize the voice. I push myself up off the cold, damp floor, stooping low so that I can shuffle toward the door. I step out and slowly stretch to my full height, moving my arms out to the sides. My back, shoulders, and neck crack loudly, and the sensation reverberates through every inch of my torso.

"Oh, man, that felt good."

I feel a hand grip my arm and drag me along what looks like a basement corridor. In addition to the guy beside me, there's another just behind. I didn't see a weapon, but there's no way he's unarmed.

I blink hard, urging my eyes to adjust, so I can see where I'm going. If I were to guess, I would say I'm about to be interrogated as to why I started a riot.

Good question...

We follow the corridor to the end and head right. There's a short, metal staircase in front of us. We climb it and step out through an open doorway into the administration section of the main building, where I was processed when I first got here.

There's a line of men waiting for me. I count six. Four guards. The warden. And Petrov, my client. The warden steps forward to meet me, and I'm pulled to a stop in front of him.

He sneers at me, openly showing his disdain. "It appears you have friends in high places, American."

I shrug my arm free of the guard's grip and crack my neck again. "I'm being released?"

"Yes. Your lawyer here has a case that you have been wrongfully imprisoned."

I glance at Petrov, who nods subtly. The Vikslavich crime

family made good on their word, it would seem.

I look at the warden and smile. "Well, I can't say I'm going to miss this place. The service is terrible, and my bedding wasn't changed once during my time here. You should say something to room service."

He glares at me. "If it were up to me, you would be back in The Hole for starting a riot."

I step to his side and lean close. "Then I'm very grateful it's not up to you."

I walk over to Petrov, who extends his hand. I shake it, and we walk over to the counter built into the left wall, where my personal belongings are waiting for me in a large plastic tray. I'm not bothered about the audience. I step out of my jumpsuit and quickly throw on my jeans, sweater, boots, and jacket. I pocket my cell and wallet, then follow Petrov out through the main door.

We leave the main building behind us and walk briskly across the graveled courtyard toward his car.

I turn to him. "I appreciate the save."

He smiles. "It's our pleasure. You did some exceptional work in there."

His American accent is impeccable.

I shrug. "Only what you paid me for."

"Don't be so humble, Adrian. Yuri's body was found in a very bad way, with a clear imprint of a Rahzva ring in his forehead. Word has spread quickly through the prison, and the Khaliskovs are out for blood. No one suspects Vikslavich involvement, and no one can place you anywhere near the cell block when it happened. That is... quite impressive."

"I did the best I could with what I had. Whatever the circumstances, I get the job done, Petrov. That's why you hired me."

We get in his car, and he starts the engine. Then he

reaches inside his jacket and produces an envelope. He hands it to me. "Your plane ticket and a fake passport, courtesy of your friend, Josh."

I smile. "I love that guy."

Petrov laughs. "Come, my friend. We must drink vodka together before you leave our country. Celebrate your success."

I lean back in the seat and stretch my legs. "Sounds good to me, Petrov. Sounds good to me."

He pulls out of the lot, the tires crunching on the gravel as we drive out through the main gate and onto the highway. I glance out the window at the ominous outline of the prison. The towering, dull structure is nothing more than a blemish on the Siberian landscape. That's got to be one of the worst places I've ever been. Still, I'm half a million dollars richer, and I think it's safe to say I've made some new friends in the Vikslavich family. Not a bad week's work, all things considered.

I glance at Petrov, who's staring intently ahead. I hope he's serving steak with this vodka. I'm starving!

THE END

A MESSAGE

Dear Reader,

Thank you for purchasing my book. If you enjoyed reading it, it would mean a lot to me if you could spare thirty seconds to leave an honest review. For independent authors like me, one review makes a world of difference!

If you want to get in touch, please visit my website, where you can contact me directly, either via e-mail or social media.

Until next time...

James P. Sumner

CLAIM YOUR FREE GIFT!

By subscribing to James P. Sumner's mailing list, you can get your hands on an exclusive novella, not available to buy anywhere else.

A Hero of War is the prequel to the bestselling Adrian Hell series, and sees the eponymous hero as a new recruit in the U.S. Army at the beginning of the Gulf War, years before he became a legendary assassin.

If you wish to claim your free gift, just visit the website below:

linktr.ee/jamespsumner

*You will receive infrequent, spam-free newsletters from the author, containing exclusive news about his books. You can unsubscribe at any time.

Printed in Great Britain
by Amazon

27322502R00148